STRANGE INVADERS

VISITORS
STRANGE INVADERS
BOOK I

Rodman Philbrick and Lynn Harnett

AN
APPLE
PAPERBACK

SCHOLASTIC INC.
New York Toronto London Auckland Sydney

Copyright © 1997 by Rodman Philbrick and Lynn Harnett.
All rights reserved. Published by Scholastic Inc.
Printed in the United States of America. 113

ISBN 0-439-06405-8

SCHOLASTIC, READ 180, APPLE PAPERBACKS, and associated logos and designs are trademarks and/or registered trademarks of Scholastic Inc.
LEXILE is a trademark of MetaMetrics, Inc.

21 22   R   14 15 16

To Deborah Harnett

1

The blaze of white light yanked me out of a sound sleep.

"Wha —!" I shot up in bed, staring around me.

In the sudden blast of brightness, all the colors seemed bleached out of my room. From my posters, gray-skinned rock stars glared at me like squirming butterflies pinned to the wall.

For an instant my room had looked like a photographic negative, as if the flash sucked the color out of everything it touched.

Weird. I'd never seen anything like it.

The night winked black again. I stared into the darkness, red spots dancing in front of my eyes. "What was that?" I wondered, feeling a tingle of fear in my blood.

CRAAAA-A-B-OOOOOOO-O-O-M!

I jumped. It was thunder, of course. First you see the lightning, then you hear the thunder. It was a storm, had to be, right? Still, it didn't sound right. But as the shuddering noise faded, I couldn't say what seemed wrong. Just something . . . odd.

Maybe it was only that I'd been woken up suddenly. Maybe there was enough of a dream left in my head to make my room look weird and strange in the night shadows.

It was only a stupid dream, Nick. Go back to sleep.

I started to slide back under the covers when — *FLASH!* — another bolt of lightning ripped across the sky. The glare burst across my room and zigzagged down the wall like a laser beam.

CRA-A-A-CK!

The thunder ripped through the night like an explosion. A bolt of lightning must have hit something nearby! Jumping out of bed, I ran to the window.

What I saw amazed me.

There was an odd, pulsing glow in the sky, in the direction of Harley Hills.

Harley Hills. Nobody lived out that way, nobody even went out into those hills much, for some reason. The whole area was kind of lonesome and spooky.

I shivered a little, peering into the weird glow, trying to see what could be making it. Could it be a fire? But there wasn't much to burn in the Harley Hills. There were hardly any trees out there, just rock.

ZAP! Suddenly another jagged burst of lightning flashed so bright it hurt my eyes. I jerked back from the window, momentarily blinded. Blinking to clear away the glary spots, I leaned forward to look out again.

Over Harley Hills, the clouds were glowing like old-fashioned lanterns with flames dancing inside. They were rolling and pitching on top of one another, as if they were alive.

This was no ordinary summer thunderstorm.

The hairs prickled along the back of my neck. The air in my room seemed to stir and grow colder.

Suddenly an icy hand grabbed the back of my neck.

"YAA-IE!"

2

Evil laughter cackled in my ear. Cold, bony fingers gripped tighter on my neck.

I whipped around, knocking the hand away and a dark figure darted just out of my reach.

"Jessica!"

It was my twin sister, and she was holding both hands against her mouth to stifle her laughter.

"Very funny, Jess," I said, rubbing my neck. "Your hands are freezing," I added, as if the coldness was the only reason I had almost jumped out of my skin. "You'd better check and make sure you've got blood in your veins and not ice water. Or antifreeze."

"Very funny," said Jessica, coming to stand next to me at the window. "The lightning woke me up, but Mom and Dad are still sleeping. Mom didn't even get up to check the windows."

"It's not raining," I pointed out.

"I know," said my sister. "That's what's so strange."

The wind whipped through the trees in the back-yard, but the air was so dry it seemed to crackle. Was it my imagination or was the strange glow over Harley Hills growing brighter?

"This is the weirdest thunderstorm I ever saw," breathed Jessie.

"You think it's weird because *you're* weird!" I taunted her.

Jessie grinned and whacked me with a pillow she snatched off my bed. I dove around her and grabbed the other pillow, but Jessie had already jumped quick as a flash out of my reach.

We were twelve and even though we were twins we didn't look anything alike. Jessie was skinny and quick and looked like Mom. She had shiny brown hair and big brown eyes and a short straight nose she stuck into everybody else's business.

I aimed the pillow at her face and heaved.

As for me, everybody says I look like my dad. That means sandy hair, blue eyes, and freckles. I was hoping someday I'd have his big, broad shoulders, too. I was bigger boned than Jess, but it was only last year I finally grew as tall as her.

Jessie caught the pillow I threw at her in midair. Now she had two. I started to duck when suddenly both of us froze. Light blazed through the window. Only this time it didn't flash like lightning and it was whiter than sun-light.

There was no thunder, just silence.

"Awesome!" Jessie whispered, her eyes open wide.

I looked out the window. What I saw made me gasp in amazement.

During our pillow fight, the strange, glowing clouds I'd seen over Harley Hills had moved closer. Much closer. Now they were directly over our house.

"What is it?" Jessie asked fearfully. "How can clouds be lit up like that? It's like they're on fire!"

"And they're all massed together in a bunch," I said, trying to keep my voice from trembling. "As if they're hiding something."

Even as I spoke, a dark shape moved deep inside the clouds.

"Nick, do you hear something?" asked Jessie.

Yes. It was a low, rumbling noise, like someone was pressing the lowest note on a church organ. The sound was so deep we could feel it more than hear it, like a vibration in our bones.

"Oooh. It makes my heart flutter," whispered Jessie.

I nodded. The sound had worked its way into my chest, too, and my stomach felt queasy.

We stared out the window as the dark shape swirled like a whirlpool inside the cloud, getting blacker by the second.

"I'm scared," said Jessie in a little-girl voice that made me shiver.

Suddenly, in the middle of the black spot, the clouds cracked open and rain poured down.

"Ow!" yelped Jessie as a fat drop hit her square in the eye. She stumbled back from the open window. "I'm blind!"

3

I slammed down the window as huge drops of rain battered against it. I'd never seen such a deluge. It was like the clouds were dumping a waterfall right on top of us.

"Are you okay, Jessie?" I asked, turning quickly to my sister.

She was wiping the water out of her eye. "I'm fine," she said, blinking. "When it hit me, the rain made my eyes sting."

Suddenly Jessie's face brightened as she stared past me. "Look!" she said, pointing out the window. "Fire-flies!"

She was right, the rain did look like fireflies, like each separate drop was glowing under its own mysterious power. We pressed up against the window, too mesmer-ized to be scared.

The whole backyard was bathed in strange rosy light

that twinkled and sparkled as the raindrops splashed all around. As the drops landed on our old swing set, they left lines of eerie light as they rolled down. Each grass blade on the lawn gave off a luminous shine. The trees dripped sparkles.

"Way cool!" I said. "It's like St. Elmo's fire."

"St. whosie's what?"

"St. Elmo's fire," I repeated. "That's what sailors in olden times called this strange glowing light they used to see on the ocean or sometimes on the mast of their ship. They thought it was some kind of curse or magic but it's just a form of static electricity — like the sparks you get on a dry day when you brush your hair. Nothing to be afraid of."

"Afraid? Are you saying I'm afraid?" Jessie stuck out her lower lip and frowned at me.

I grinned back at her. "You're a girl," I said. "Girls are supposed to be scared."

She drew herself up and glared at me. "No way!"

"Way!"

"I'm your twin," Jessie reminded me. "If I'm scared, then so are you."

She was right. Lots of times we did share feelings. She was right about something else, too. I *was* kind of scared. But I was even more excited than I was afraid. I wanted to know what was going on with these glowing clouds that weren't like any storm clouds I'd ever seen.

"There's only one way to prove you're not scared," I said.

"What's that?" By the angry glow in her eyes, I could see Jessie would take any challenge.

I had to raise my voice a little to be heard above the pounding rain. "We go outside."

4

The kitchen was filled with strange, flickering light from the glowing rain.

"It's totally weird that Mom and Dad could sleep through this," said Jessie, peering doubtfully out the back door at what looked like a wall of shining water. "Maybe we should wake them," she suggested.

"Yeah, and maybe they wouldn't let us go outside. Maybe you'd like that," I said sarcastically.

Just as I had hoped, she got all huffy and yanked open the door. "We're going to get wet," Jessie predicted, hunching her shoulders. But even as she spoke, the rain stopped, as if it had been turned off with a switch. As if whatever caused this weird storm wanted us to go outside.

I stepped past Jessie and walked out into the night. "Wow!"

Every twig and leaf, every line of the house and our old rusting swing set was outlined in zingy light, like neon. Pearls of light still dripped from the trees. It was beautiful — but something about it made my skin crawl.

"Oh, no," cried Jessie. "It's going away."

She was right. The light was beginning to fade. It went slowly, like a flashlight with a dying battery.

Jessie darted back into the kitchen and grabbed an empty glass jar, the kind we used to use for catching fireflies. She stooped and began to scoop up some of the rainwater from the grass. "Maybe if we seal it up we can keep some of the glow inside," she said, screwing on the cap and shaking the jar to watch the light slosh up the sides.

I knelt down and ran my finger through a fading puddle. The water was cool. I put my finger to my lips to taste it. The rainwater had an odd but not unpleasant taste. Kind of like cinnamon.

"Don't, Nick!" warned Jessie. "Better not taste that stuff. It could be some kind of pollution. Like acid rain, only worse."

She was right. Jessie often was. She had a sensible streak. But, of course, it was too late. I spit on the ground but still felt the spicy flavor on my tongue.

"Look," cried Jessie. "The clouds are going away!"

Above our house the sky was clear and stars were visible. The big mass of clouds, clumped up like piles of cotton candy, was moving back toward the hills. The glow was fainter. I had the funniest feeling that we had imagined the whole thing.

But when the clouds reached Harley Hills they seemed to settle over the top of the highest peak. And then the spooky hills began to glow as if there was a fire deep inside the earth.

The hairs stood up all over my body.

"What's going on?" I breathed to nobody in particular.

"Could it be a reflection from the clouds doing that?" Jessie wondered.

"Maybe," I said. "But I've got a real strange feeling it's something much weirder than just a reflection in the clouds."

"What do you mean?" Jessie asked.

"Maybe we just had a visitor," I said. "A visitor not of this earth."

5

Inside our house it was as silent as a tomb. Jess and I crept up the stairs, careful not to wake Mom and Dad, and went to our rooms.

Before shutting her door, Jess glared at me and whispered, "You're just trying to scare me, right?"

There were times when we tried to scare each other, but this wasn't one of them. When I got back inside my room, I pulled the shades down. The last thing I wanted to do was lie there in the dark with the glow from Harley Hills reflected on the walls. Making my room look strange and creepy.

Just to make sure, I pulled the blanket over my head and squeezed my eyes shut. Go to sleep, I told myself. When you wake up everything will be back to normal.

Except I never got back to sleep.

Lying there with my head under the covers, I could hear every little thing inside our house. The bed-creak noise as my sister tossed and turned in her room. A faucet drip . . . drip . . . dripping in the bathroom. The refrigerator cycling on and off in the kitchen. The creaking of a door hinge.

Wait. A door hinge? That meant somebody was up and moving around. And yet I hadn't heard footsteps, so how could anybody be opening a door?

A small, muffled thump came from somewhere downstairs on the first floor.

I sat bolt upright in bed, straining to hear.

Thump . . . thump . . .

There it was again. A noise I'd never before heard at night. I listened so hard my ears seemed to get hot. So why was I shivering?

Thump . . . thump . . .

Someone was in my house. Or some*thing*.

At just that moment my bedroom door opened silently.

It was here, in my room. Coming to get me.

6

"Nick, do you hear that?" my sister hissed.

She was wrapped in her blanket; that's why she'd looked so strange coming through the door.

Thump . . . thump . . .

The faint noise was still there, coming from downstairs.

"What do you think it is?" I asked.

"I was hoping you'd know," Jessie whispered. "I think we should wake Mom and Dad."

Why hadn't I thought of that? What were parents for, if not to check out scary noises in the night? My dad would grab his flashlight and go to investigate and then in a few minutes he'd come back upstairs and announce it was nothing. A loose shutter. A tree brushing the side of the house. Nothing to worry about.

Just thinking about my parents made me feel better.

"We'll go wake them right now," I said, getting out of bed.

Jess followed me to their bedroom door.

Knock-knock. "Dad!" I hissed. "Mom!"

I tried knocking louder. No one answered, so I pushed open the door and entered. This was an emergency. We *had* to wake them up.

"Oh, no," Jessie said quietly. "What do we do now?"

The bedroom was empty. Mom and Dad weren't there.

Thump . . . thump . . .

The noise was slightly louder when I got to the top of the stairs. There was no choice. We *had* to go down and check it out.

Something was deeply wrong. First, the eerie storm, the strange clouds over Harley Hills, the rain that glowed in the dark. Then our parents disappearing from their room. No way could we just ignore everything and go back to sleep.

So I started down the stairs. Jessie was right behind me, hanging on to my pajama top. I knew she was scared, but it made it easier, having her there.

Thump . . . thump . . .

Something about that noise was familiar, but I couldn't put my finger on it.

"It's not coming from the kitchen or the living room," Jess whispered when we got to the bottom of the stairs.

No, it was coming from somewhere deeper. I thought I knew where, and just the idea of it made me shiver.

17

The basement.

Thump . . . thump . . .

The muffled noise was coming up through the floor. From deep in the basement.

"Maybe it's the furnace," I said. "The furnace makes weird noises sometimes, right?"

"Not like that," said Jess. "And how come Mom and Dad aren't in their bedroom? Something bad has happened, Nick."

"It's probably nothing," I said. But I didn't believe it.

"There's only one way to find out," suggested Jess.

"Right," I said. "Let's do it."

We headed for the basement door, with me leading the way. I was acting brave on the outside, but inside my stomach felt like a chunk of frozen roadkill.

The basement door was at the end of the hallway. I tried flicking on the hall light, but it was burned out. I knew, because I was supposed to change the bulb, but had never got around to it. Served me right, having to come down here in the dark.

Thump . . . thump . . .

"It's louder," whispered Jess.

She was right. It was louder and it was definitely coming from deep in the basement.

I stopped short right at the door. My sister bumped into me from behind, almost knocking us both down. "Careful!" I hissed.

Cautiously I put my ear against the door panel.

Thump . . . thump . . .

The noise was clear as a bell. And I was pretty sure I knew what it was. The sound a shovel makes as it scoops up the dirt.

Someone was down there in the basement, digging.

7

It was Jessie who opened the basement door. For some reason my hand wouldn't work — probably because it was shaking so much.

Eeeeeeeeeeeeeeeeeeek.

That's the noise the hinges made as the door swung open. Beyond the doorway, the stairs led down into the darkness.

THUMP . . . THUMP . . .

It was much louder and very distinct. The sound of a shovel chewing into the earth.

I went down to the first step, my legs disappearing into the shadows. "Mom?" I called out. "Dad?"

Nothing. No reply. Just the steady, maddening noise of shoveling.

I was so scared inside that I was sure my legs wouldn't work. But despite the fear, my feet slipped down to the next step. And the next. I felt like I was vanishing into the darkness. But my legs kept on going. Taking me down into the basement. Closer and closer to the sound of someone digging.

Or some*thing* digging.

Something that had come in from the weird storm in the sky. Something made from glowing rain. Something that had stolen our parents right out of their bedroom. Something that was digging a grave in the basement.

I wanted to scream, but my mouth wouldn't open. I wanted to run, but my feet kept going down the steps.

THUMP . . . THUMP . . .

I knew there was a flashlight on a shelf near the bottom of the stairs. My dad always kept one there, for emergencies. If I could just get to that flashlight, I'd be safe. That's what I kept telling myself: *Get to the flashlight, get to the flashlight.*

I got to where the flashlight should have been, but it wasn't there. I was fumbling around, searching for it, when my fingers touched something that shouldn't have been there.

Something alive.

I wanted to scream, but nothing came out of my mouth. And before I could move, the thing I'd touched came out of the dark and grabbed me. Grabbed me so hard I couldn't move. It was strong, stronger than anything human.

This time I knew it wasn't Jess, because she was standing at the top of the stairs and screaming her head off.

"MOM! DAD! HELP!"

Suddenly a white light blasted me in the eyes. I couldn't see a thing, just the hot white light burning into my brain.

Then, just as quickly as it had come, the beam of light flicked away. A moment later the regular basement light was turned on, and Jessie came running down the stairs, her face filled with a look of wonder.

"MOM! DAD!" she yelled.

I twisted around and got a look at the thing that was holding me.

But it wasn't a thing, it was my mom. And she was holding the flashlight I'd been looking for. "Hold-still," she said. "Do-not-move!"

My sudden relief at finding my mom stopped short. Because it wasn't my mother's familiar, friendly voice coming out of her mouth. It was like the voice of a stranger.

"Mom," I said. "Are you okay?"

"I-am-a-normal-human-being," she said, enunciating each syllable like she was learning a new language. "I-am-normal, perfectly-normal."

Slowly she released me and stepped back.

That's when Dad stepped out of the shadow. He was holding a shovel and his eyes were as cold and bright as the moon.

8

Mom and Dad marched us up the stairs, out of the basement.

"This-location-is-off-limits," said Mom in her strange new voice.

Dad snapped a padlock on the door. "Do-not-violate-this-space," he said.

His voice was like Mom's. It sounded familiar, but somehow different. Stiff and awkward like he was processing a new language.

"It-is-time-for-your-sleep-interval, is-it-not?" said Dad.

My sister looked like her eyes were going to bug out. "What's wrong with you guys?" she demanded. "What were you doing down there in the basement? You didn't even have the lights on!"

Mom and Dad looked at each other. Then Dad shrugged his shoulders and said, "Our-activity-is-none-of-your-business. You-are-children, we-are-adults. You-must-obey-us."

We didn't have any choice. Jessie and I trudged along with our parents right behind us.

If they really were my mom and dad.

"Go-to-your-cubicles," said Dad in his strange new voice.

Jessie nudged me as we walked down the hallway, heading for our bedrooms. "Did you hear that?" she whispered. And gave me one of her scrunched-up-nose looks that meant we both understood without having to explain it in words: Something was terribly wrong.

When I got back to my bedroom, I shut and locked the door. Not that I really thought a locked door would make me safe, but somehow it made me feel better. Just like it made me feel better to pull the covers over my head, like I used to do when I was a little kid.

I figured I'd never be able to sleep again, but there's something about being scared that makes you tired, and before long I nodded off, dreaming about a strange glow in the sky that had turned my parents into aliens.

"Only a dream," I mumbled into my pillow. "Please let it be only a dream."

I woke up hot and clammy. The sun blazed through the window shades. I lay there for a moment, trying to remember what had happened the night before.

Something about a storm. The basement. A bad dream.

I sat up so fast my head got dizzy. There was a gummy, spicy taste in my mouth. Then a picture of the glowing raindrops flashed into my head, and I swung my feet to the floor.

It was only a dream, I told myself. So get out of bed and prove it.

"Nick! Are you up!" Jessie's voice hissed at my door.

"Come on in."

She rattled the door knob. Right, I'd locked it the night before.

"Hey," I said when her impish face appeared.

"Are you thinking what I'm thinking?" my sister said.

It wasn't just a casual question. We were twins and we often had the same thought at exactly the same moment.

I nodded. "We imagined it," I said. "We got spooked by a weird storm, and we imagined that our parents had been taken over by aliens."

Jess nodded in eager agreement. "How dumb can you get, huh?"

And so we went downstairs for breakfast convinced that everything was back to normal.

We couldn't have been more wrong.

9

I knew something wasn't right before we got to the bottom of the stairs.

"I don't smell any breakfast cooking," I said.

Jessie stopped. She turned to me, frowning. "You're right," she said. "But Mom always cooks us breakfast. And how come she didn't wake us up?" She jammed her hands in the pockets of her jeans and turned in a slow circle, sniffing. "Does the air in here seem funny to you? Too thick or something?"

"Nooo," I said slowly. "Just too quiet."

Jessie started down the hall toward the kitchen. "Mom and Dad must be in the backyard."

But they weren't in the backyard. Jessie stepped into the kitchen and stopped so suddenly I bumped into her. "Hey, guys!" she said. "Good morning!"

Nobody answered.

Then I saw them. Mom and Dad were sitting at the kitchen table opposite each other. They sat so straight and stiff they looked like wooden statues. They didn't even look at us.

Weird.

"Hey, Mom, how come you didn't call us for breakfast?" I asked. My voice sounded loud. But she didn't hear. She just stared at some spot over Dad's shoulder.

Jessie clutched my arm and I could feel she was as freaked as I was. I pushed past her and went over to the table, banging a chair hard on the floor. "Mom, Dad, what's up?" My voice cracked.

Mom shuddered. A ripple passed over her face. Her head jerked toward me and her eyes locked onto mine. Her eyes were hard, like glass marbles. Then something slithered in the depths. My heart froze. I let go of the chair and it banged again.

"Yes?" Mom asked in a strange voice. "What-is-it-that-you-want?"

I stuttered, choking on my own breath. My mom sounded like a robot. "Breakfast?" I squeaked.

She frowned. It was like she was trying to remember what the word meant. I felt frozen to the spot. But I wanted to flee — from my own mother!

"Breakfast," she repeated finally in the same monotone voice. "You'll-have-to-help-yourself. I'm-busy."

"Busy," said another voice. Dad! I jumped at the unfamiliar sound of his voice. Turning to look at him, I was horrified to see the same strange slithering motion in his eyes that I'd seen in Mom's. Then it was gone and his eyes were just flat with no expression at all, like chips of ice.

Jessie let out a little yelp from behind me. "Mom, Dad," she cried. "Are you all right? What's wrong?"

Neither of them seemed to hear her. They heard the words, all right, but not the distress in her voice. "Everything's-fine," said Dad in his toneless new voice. He got up from the table, rising slowly and mechanically from his seat.

"Perfectly-normal," said Mom, sounding like a computer programmed for cheerful. She got up, too, and I backed away from them both, almost tripping over my own feet.

"We-have-things-to-do," said Dad. He walked stiffly across the kitchen, opened the basement door, and disappeared down the stairs.

Mom followed. But at the basement door, she turned. Her eyes locked onto me. "Do-not-fear-us, little-ones," she said. "We-are-your-parents-and-we-know-best."

10

"That's it," Jessie said. "We've got to find out what really happened last night."

My sister didn't have to tell me what she had in mind. I already knew.

"Harley Hills," I breathed.

We got our bikes out of the shed. I think we were both a little scared by the idea of Harley Hills, that spooky place they sometimes call "the badlands." But what choice did we have? We had to find out what had happened and why our parents were suddenly acting so . . . changed.

"You'd never know there was a major storm last night," observed Jessie as we pedaled down the sidewalk.

I nodded. Everything was dry. And no sparkles in the grass or drifting down from the trees, either.

"It's like the storm never happened," I said. "Except we know it did, right?"

"Right," said Jessie, catching my mood. "Harley Hills, here we come!"

We headed north out of town. Which didn't take long. Harleyville wasn't a very big town and we lived on the outskirts. As we pedaled up the bike path along Route 33, we passed a few houses. But no one was outside even though it was a beautiful, sunny day.

Pretty soon we left the houses behind and the woods closed in on either side of the road. Usually I liked this ride. The sun filters through the trees, making patterns on the road. And with no houses in sight, you can almost believe you're in the wilderness. But today I wished there were a few more people around. There was a brooding, lonesome feel to the woods that gave me the creeps.

A little further on, the forest thinned out and we came to an area of old, abandoned fields strewn with boulders and caved-in fence posts. Beyond them we could see the barren hills looming against the sky.

Without speaking, we turned off onto the dirt track that led up into the hills. Almost nothing grew here. Just some weeds and scrubby looking bushes.

Sometimes Jessie and I and some of the other kids would pretend we were riding into the Old West, into a hard land of outlaws and posses. But today the hills just looked creepy and desolate. The few trees were crooked and spindly and lonely-looking. The bare, chalky hills looked like sleeping, humpbacked giants. Boulders rose up like menacing trolls.

The Harley Hills were the three tallest hills in the middle of the badlands. The center one, Harley Hill itself, was the highest. People said it was named for an old hermit who lived on its summit long before there was a town. The hill spread a long, dark shadow over the rocky ground.

We both stopped at the edge of that shadow, reluctant to go further. There was something — a jagged, darker spot in the middle of the shadow that didn't seem right. It looked different but I couldn't say how.

"Did it suddenly get a whole lot colder?" asked Jessie, close beside me.

"No," I said. "I'm not cold. We're right in the sun."

"Then why am I shivering?" asked Jessie. "And why are you shivering?"

I didn't want to tell her. I thought it would sound silly. But there was a lump of dread in the pit of my stomach. I scanned the hill, looking for something, anything. But there was no one there. Nothing moved, not even a rabbit.

But I couldn't shake off the strong feeling that someone — or something — was watching us.

Suddenly Jessie gave a yelp of surprise. Or fear. "Look!" she cried. "That must be where the lightning struck!"

I looked where she was pointing and suddenly realized that the black patch wasn't part of the shadow at all. It was a huge slash of scorched earth. I mean, burned!

"But it's as big as a football field," I said slowly.

"Could lightning do that?" Jessie wondered. "Come on, let's check it out."

"No, Jessie!" I said sharply. "We need to be careful about this."

But she was already scrambling over the rocks and rough ground. One part of my twin sister was smart and sensible, always thinking. The other part was like this, stubborn and totally fixated. "Jessie, wait!" I called, but she acted like she didn't hear me.

So I went after her, even though I felt in my bones it was a bad idea.

When I caught up with her, Jessie was kneeling right in the middle of the strange, scorched area. "Look, it goes right up into the hill, like an arrow pointing the way," she said excitedly. "I think we should follow it, see where it leads."

Her eyes were wide and eager — and scared, too, though she would never admit it. It was a look I recognized. It meant she was going to follow the scorched ground, no matter what. Being scared just made her that much more determined.

There was no point arguing.

The rocks under our feet felt weird, brittle, like shells on a beach. The ground crunched as we walked. It smelled a little like concrete after a rainstorm, only burnt and very dry. Cool, too. Although the climb was kind of steep, we were both chilly and shivering.

It felt like the ground was sucking the heat out of us, right through the bottom of our sneakers.

As we climbed, the scorched ground got narrower and darker as if the heat had been more intense the higher we went. The shape was like an arrow pointing the way. But to where?

"Weird, huh?" said Jessie, as we reached the top.

The burn mark ended in a sharp point. At the end was a jagged, blackened area shaped like a starburst.

"It looks like the lightning struck exactly here," I said, laying my hand in the center of the star shape, "and then scorched all the way down the hill."

"That's strange," breathed Jessica.

"Sure is," I agreed.

"No. I don't mean that." Her voice was oddly flat. "I mean the town. Harleyville."

"What about it?" I pulled my hand from the center of the "star," realizing it had turned ice-cold.

"I can't see it from here," said Jessie.

I stood up, rubbing my numb hand. That's when I noticed that Jessie looked terrified.

"It's not there," she said. "It's like the whole world has disappeared!"

11

Jessie was right. The town, our home, our friends — it was as if everything had suddenly vanished.

We were up high on Harley Hill, facing south. Harleyville should have been in plain sight. Only it wasn't there. I couldn't see a single house or church or gas station or playground or person. Just empty badlands, stretching on forever.

I blinked, shook my head, rubbed my eyes. Nothing changed. The town had disappeared.

"Maybe there's something wrong with our sense of direction," I said to Jessie in a voice that sounded normal. "Maybe we got turned around somehow."

She looked at me doubtfully, but we both ran to the other side of the hilltop, our feet sliding on loose stones and kicking up dust. When we stopped, Jessie let out a little whimper.

The view was exactly the same from this side. Lumpy, hunched-looking brown hills, dark, impenetrable gullies, long, cold shadows. No town. No buildings. No road or cars or anything.

"Look, we know the town is there," I said, trying to sound reasonable. "Towns don't just disappear. It must be an optical illusion. Something to do with the sun and the shadows."

"Are you serious?" said Jessie, squinting at me.

"The way the hills block the sunlight," I said desperately.

"It could be the clouds, too," said Jessie, nodding. "Sunlight bounces off the hills and reflects back and back again like a bunch of mirrors set up looking at each other. So all we see is hills and more hills."

"Yeah, that's it." My eyes knew what they saw but my brain was doing flip-flops scrambling for an explanation.

Jessica grabbed my sleeve. "What's that?" she asked. "Listen."

I stiffened at the faint crunching sound of footsteps.

"Someone's climbing the hill after us," Jessie whispered urgently. "I think we should hide."

We ducked behind a boulder that was taller than us. Pebbles skittered down the hillside. The footsteps grew louder.

Crunch, crunch.

My muscles stiffened in fear. What should we do? Who could it be?

Nobody ever came up here. Nobody human.

35

My heart began to lurch in time with the steadily approaching steps. I looked around, trying to figure an escape route. Jessie looked pretty scared. Her whole body was trembling.

CRUNCH, CRUNCH.

The footsteps were much louder now. Coming closer, closer. I could hear breathing. No, it was panting, like an animal. A big animal.

Jessie's hand tightened on my arm. I was about to signal her to run when the footsteps stopped. All we could hear was the raspy breathing.

Then whatever it was started moving again and my heart sank. The steps sounded determined. The thing was heading right for our hiding place.

We were trapped.

12

CRUNCH!

Charred stones pulverized under a heavy foot and went cascading down the hillside. Jessie's nails dug into my arm. Our only way out was to run right in front of the thing.

CRUNCH, CRUNCH!

It stopped right beside our boulder. As if it could hear our pounding hearts.

WHOOSH!

It let out a huge breath of air. In my mind, I imagined a fire-breathing monster, ready to pounce on the two puny humans.

Then it spoke.

"Wow! Massive!" it said in a deep, froggy voice.

Jessie's hand fell away from my arm. She stepped out into the open. "Frasier!" she exclaimed. "You scared the daylights out of us."

"Cool!" he said.

Frasier Wellington was our good bud, same age as us. He was bigger than me but kind of clumsy. He grinned, showing the gap between his front teeth. His eyes got big behind his thick glasses. "Scared you, huh?"

"Not exactly," I said, rolling my eyes as if the idea was ridiculous. "It sounded like a herd of elephants coming up the hill, so we thought we ought to check it out before showing ourselves."

"What are you doing up here?" asked Jessie suspiciously.

"Same as you," said Frasier, bending over to examine a burned rock. "Checking out the storm damage."

"So you heard it, too," said Jessie, looking relieved. Frasier lived right next door to us. "Did it wake you up?"

"Sure. Who could sleep through that?" He let the rock fall to the ground and picked up another one. Frasier was a rock hound. He collected rocks and displayed them on shelves in his room. "Except for my parents. They'll sleep through anything."

"Your parents slept through the whole thing?" asked Jessie in a strange, tense voice.

But Frasier was too absorbed to notice. He put the burned rock in his pocket. "Yup," he said. "They sure did."

"Hey, Frase," I said, shooting Jessie a look. I didn't want to talk about our parents. "Did you notice anything, um, peculiar about that storm?"

Frasier shrugged his shoulders, poked his glasses

back up his nose. "You mean like flashes of weird light but no actual lightning bolts? Glowing clouds? Glowing rain? Kind of a funny vibration in the air?" He squinted like he does when he's thinking. "I guess that about covers the peculiar stuff. Except for this incredible expanse of scorched earth. Now this is *really* peculiar."

I felt relieved that Frasier had seen the same things we had. At least our house hadn't been totally singled out by whatever it was.

"What about the view?" asked Jessie. "Did you happen to look toward town from up here?"

Frasier rubbed the top of his crew cut with his palm, a gesture that meant he was uneasy. "A simple, atmospheric inversion," he said with blustery confidence. "Like a mirage."

That sounded like a good explanation until I remembered that Frasier liked to throw around big words when he didn't know what he was talking about.

"This is really cool," said Frasier, pointing along the starburst area. He was changing the subject, also not a good sign. He dropped to his hands and knees and began sniffing around the scorched center. He looked like a nervous terrier with glasses.

"What are you doing?" asked Jessie.

"Identifying the odor," he answered, turning his head to squint up at us. "Didn't you notice how strong it is? It's ozone."

"Ozone? What's ozone?" I asked. Frasier's basically a cool guy, but sometimes he's like a human computer, he knows so much. He wasn't blustering and talking fast this time, so I knew he really had discovered something.

"Ozone is created when a strong electrical current passes through the air," he explained, sniffing the points of the star shape. "Some of the oxygen gets changed to ozone. You can smell it after a storm."

"So you think what we saw was an ordinary storm?" asked Jessie, sounding hopeful.

Frasier grinned and got up, dusting off his jeans. "I didn't say that. Lightning isn't the only thing that can make ozone."

"Oh? What else?" I asked, pretty sure I didn't really want to know.

"A UFO," Frasier announced triumphantly. "The smell of ozone is often reported following the sighting of an unidentified flying object."

"What!" Jessie's eyes followed the path of scorched earth that widened down the length of the hill.

"A spaceship," said Frasier, nodding happily. "We may have ourselves a visitor!"

All of a sudden I felt a burning sensation on the top of my head, like something with hot eyes was staring at me. One thing I knew for sure, human eyes didn't feel like that, no matter how they stared.

My mind flashed back to that horrible scene in the

basement last night. And the flickering movement I'd seen in my parents' eyes this morning. And the crawly sensation when my mom stared at me before going down into the basement.

I whirled, thinking to catch sight of whatever was watching, and far above us a shadow moved. I shouted and ducked as a shower of pebbles pelted down from above. A shape launched itself into the air and dove straight at my head.

13

A piercing cry rang in my ears. I covered my head and crouched. A sound like a helicopter propeller beat the air.

"Look out!" Frasier shouted as he and Jessie dropped down beside me.

The shriek split the air again. I felt something hostile slap the top of my head. Gusts of wind blasted my face, making my eyes water.

"Wow," cried Frasier. "Haliaeetus leucocephalus!"

Haliwhatsis? Was this the alien? Were we going to be snatched right off the top of Harley Hill, never to be heard from again?

I rolled behind the boulder where we'd hid before, dragging Jessie with me. "Frasier," I shouted. "Over here, quick! Before it comes back."

We huddled, covering our heads, but Frasier didn't come. Everything was quiet. Had Frasier been snatched?

Or was he lying on the ground injured? I had to go see. Cautiously I moved forward and peered around the rock.

Frasier was standing, looking up into the sky, shielding his eyes with his hand.

"Frasier!" I hissed. "What are you doing?"

"Did you see that?" he said excitedly. "That was a haliaeetus leucocephalus. Latin name for a bald eagle."

"An eagle?" I said. "We got zoomed by an eagle?"

"It was huge," Frasier said, nodding. "I read they were nesting here again, but this is the first one I've seen. Awesome, wasn't it?"

"Real awesome," said Jessie sarcastically. "It obviously doesn't want us here and I agree. This place is creepy. I'm leaving."

"But what about the burn mark?" asked Frasier, dismayed. "Don't you want to investigate? See if we can find proof of a UFO?"

Jessie stalked past him, then turned back angrily. "Right now I want to see if we can find proof of a town," she said. "Last time I looked, it wasn't there."

I felt a little queasy as we headed back to our bikes. It was bad enough that our parents were acting weird. And I still had the uncomfortable feeling of unseen, unfriendly eyes boring into my back.

But if the town had really disappeared —? I couldn't even stand to think about that.

None of us spoke much as we pedaled back toward Harleyville. But then we rounded the first bend and saw the Wilsons' house right where it was supposed to be. And then more houses and there was the church steeple rising over the town.

All of a sudden we were all laughing and talking at once although nobody talked about the crazy fears we'd been having.

It was peanut butter and jelly for lunch. Mom and Dad were still in the basement. They didn't even answer when we called out that we were home. The big shiny padlock on the basement door was like a warning.

Finally, when it got dark, Jessie went and banged on the door. "Mom," she yelled. "What's for dinner?"

"We're-working-on-a-special-project," Dad called back. And then Mom shouted, "You're-old-enough-to-fend-for-yourselves!"

Jessie and I just looked at each other in shock. We were always arguing that we were old enough to do things for ourselves, and Mom was always arguing that we weren't. So what could we do?

We made peanut butter and jelly sandwiches for dinner. Lunch, okay, but dinner? What about the balanced diet Mom was always insisting on?

Mom and Dad didn't eat at all.

Afterwards we settled in front of the TV. It should have been a luxury. We could watch anything, for as long as we wanted. Usually Dad monitored what we watched and two shows was our limit.

But we couldn't concentrate. Every time there was a thump or a bump in the basement below us, we jumped. Finally we just went to bed early, but I don't think either of us slept much.

The next morning I woke up at my usual time. I threw off the bedclothes and went to the window. Another bright, sunny day. I breathed deep, smelling the fresh, clean air. All yesterday's creepy feelings seemed blown away in the breeze.

The strange thunderstorm and the pink, glowing rain were like a dream. And why had Jessie and I been so upset about Mom and Dad? So they were working on some big surprise in the basement. Why was that such a big deal?

Maybe they'd finished it last night and today they would show us what they'd been doing.

I pulled on my clothes fast. I was famished. Mom was right — peanut butter and jelly weren't enough fuel for a growing boy.

Heading downstairs, I thought today might be a good day to play baseball. Harley Hills and the badlands had always been spooky, even before the strange storm. If we didn't want to get weirded out, then all we had to do was not go there. Simple.

Jessie was already in the kitchen, seated at the table.

Mom and Dad were nowhere around. Dad must have gone to work early, I figured.

Then the back door banged and Mom came in with a big bright box. "Breakfast," she announced, dumping the box on the table.

"Doughnuts!" I said, snagging a sugary jelly doughnut out of the box. "Cool, Mom!" I bit down and raspberry ooze filled my mouth.

"Yeah, this is a first, isn't it, Nick?" Jessie observed, with an edge to her voice.

I looked at Mom standing beside the table. She was looking off into space intently as if listening to something we couldn't hear.

"You don't usually let us have doughnuts for breakfast, Mom," said Jessie pointedly. "As a matter of fact this is the first time ever."

Mom blinked. Something moved in her eyes — something that had no business being there. But then she looked away and I wasn't sure what I'd seen.

The scrumptious doughnut suddenly went stale in my mouth. Something wasn't right here.

"Time-for-a-change," said Mom, sounding stiff and bright as if she were trying to sound cheerful but didn't know how. "Change-is-good. Change-is-normal. Perfectly-normal." She turned on her heel and headed for the basement door, fishing a key out of her pocket and fitting it to the padlock.

Jessie made a disgusted noise and turned her back. The lock snapped open but instead of heading into the basement, Mom turned and stared at Jessie.

Her eyes bored into the back of Jessie's skull but Jessie just sat huddled, totally unaware. A chill ran down my backbone. I felt a buzzing in the air, a ringing filling my ears.

I jumped up, trying to break Mom's concentration or get Jessie's attention but it was like they were locked in a private tunnel away from me. Jessie didn't move a muscle.

Then, slowly, a few strands of Jessie's hair began to rise up from her head, then a few more. They waved in the air like snakes all by themselves. I gulped air but I couldn't make a sound.

Then very slowly, as if she didn't know what she was doing, Jessie started to stand up. She rose from her chair as if she were being tugged by her waving locks of hair. Her face was frozen, like a photograph.

The air was thick. I felt like I was gasping for breath in a bowl of soup. I tried to shout, but no sound came. Panicking, I flung myself across the table, kicking over my chair, which landed on the tile floor with a crash.

Jessie jumped. "Sheesh, Nick," she said. "You're so clumsy. If you want another doughnut, all you have to do is say so."

I thought I heard a grunt of anger and disappointment from Mom. But when I looked over, the basement door was closing behind her. There was the snick of the bolt on the inside, then her footsteps headed down.

Jessie scratched the back of her head. "I think there's a mosquito in here," she said. "It just bit my scalp."

Something metal clanked on the basement floor.

Jessie made a face. "Let's get out of here," she said a second before I was about to say the same thing.

When we were out in the yard, Jessie turned to face me. "There's something wrong," she said, scratching her head absently.

"Hey, what's so bad about doughnuts for breakfast?" I said, but my voice was shaking too much for the fake cheerfulness to work.

"It's not the doughnuts. It's Mom. She's acting like the Energizer Bunny."

"Maybe she had too much coffee," I suggested.

Jessie rolled her eyes. "She didn't have any coffee. Nothing to eat either." Jessie's shoulders slumped. "Get serious, Nick. Something's wrong and you know it! We need to find out what it is. So we can do something about it."

"I like having peanut butter for dinner and doughnuts for breakfast," I said stubbornly, more scared than I wanted to admit. I peered into the mass of Jessie's hair, to see if there was a mark on her scalp.

The doughnut sat like a stone in my stomach. If I told Jessie I'd seen her hair waving in the air while Mom stared like Jessie was some kind of fascinating experi- ment — well, she'd flip.

And the more I thought about it, outside in the sun- shine on an ordinary day, the more I realized how ridiculous I was being.

Static electricity made Jessie's hair stick up. And Mom had been staring at her because Jessie was acting so sulky. That was all.

But Jessie would go for the alien theory for sure. An alien takeover! Crazy!

Unless it happened to be true.

14

"Hey, weenies!" Frasier skidded up on his mountain bike, saving me from having to argue with Jessie.

"Whrrooom!" he said, stopping an inch in front of us, his front wheel lifting into the air. "How do you like my full-throated, double-barrel exhaust pipes? Neat, right?"

Frasier had attached balloons to his tires so they banged against the spokes making a cool noise, if I cared about that sort of thing — which at the moment I didn't.

"What's the matter?" he asked, noticing our stiff expressions.

"It's my mom," Jessie burst out, her voice breaking. "She's acting so, so — different."

"Different?" asked Frasier, cocking his head. Binoculars hung on a strap around his neck.

"Strange," said Jessie. "Weird." She knew that telling Frasier about the doughnuts wouldn't cut it. His mom let him eat just about anything.

Frasier shrugged. "Parents are always acting strange and weird. That's no reason to get bummed out," he said. "Take my mom. Last night I stayed up till two in the morning playing computer games, and she didn't say a word. Usually she'd go ballistic. But last night I didn't even hear her go to bed."

He started polishing his binoculars on his bright green T-shirt. "Parents go through phases," he continued, like he knew what he was talking about. "She'll snap out of it in a day or two. Unfortunately. Then it'll be back to normal time. Don't worry, Jessie, it's all perfectly normal."

Jessie grabbed her hair in her fists and screamed, "Don't say that!"

Frasier stepped back, startled. "What's with your sister, man?" he whispered to me.

"She's just upset," I said. "Didn't, um, get enough sleep."

Jessie shot me a dirty look. "I'm going to get my bike," she said and strode off toward the shed where we kept them.

"Yeah? Or maybe she ate too many chocolate doughnuts." Frasier grinned. "Can you spare one for a bud?"

As he chomped away on the last doughnut, Jessie came back with her bike. "Better get your wheels, Nick," Frasier suggested, wiping crumbs off his face. "Time to go."

"Go?" I asked. "Go where?"

Frasier stuck the bike helmet back on his head and tightened the strap. "Back to Harley Hills," he said. "Where else?"

My stomach churned around those doughnuts, but I knew he was right. We had to go back. We had to find out what had happened in those strange hills.

We started wheeling our bikes out to the road. But as we passed the garage, I heard something. I stopped.

Clank.

There it was again. Coming from inside the garage.

"Wait," I called out. "I think your cat might be in our garage again, Frasier. My dad must have left the door open when he went to work. There's paint and stuff in there. I'll get her out and close the door."

"Hurry up. We'll wait here."

I laid my bike down and headed for the garage, ignoring the prickly feeling crawling up the back of my neck.

Clank!

The noise sounded kind of loud for a cat. Maybe a raccoon had gotten in there. But as I got closer, I saw something really strange. My dad's car! It was still in the garage. But if the car was there, then how had he gotten to work?

I moved closer, a little slower now. I heard shuffling noises, and then I saw something big and bulky move deep in the shadows in the back of the garage where it was darkest. It was much too big to be a cat or a raccoon.

Swallowing, I thought about turning back. But I could just imagine telling Frasier I'd heard noises in the garage and was too chicken to check it out. Right. Weenyville for sure.

Taking a few more steps, I squinted to see into the darkness. I was almost at the open door, but it was so bright outside I could hardly see in at all.

Something growled.

"GRRRRRRRR."

I leaped about a foot, my heard pounding. If I could reach the door I could pull it down quick, trapping whatever it was inside. Moving silently, I crept forward, my eyes on the door handle. It was a good plan. Whatever was in there was way in the back, unaware of me.

I jumped for the door handle, snagged it. Smoothly the door slid on its tracks. Something bellowed and a face swam out of the blackness right in front of me. It had big teeth and they were aimed at my throat.

Then the door caught and snagged, halfway down. I had failed! I tried to run, then tripped over a rock and went sprawling.

I was dead meat for sure.

15

Something shaggy and huge was emerging from the garage. I felt paralyzed. All I could do was wait for it to get me.

No! I had to fight. Panicky, I ran my hand over the grass, looking for the rock that had tripped me. I got my fingers on it, gripped, and pulled. But that rock was stuck tight.

"Nick! What-are-you-doing?"

The shaggy thing stood up and suddenly I recognized my dad. His hair stood up all over his head in messy spikes. He was wearing some big, thick, grungy coat I'd never seen before. And it was about eighty degrees out.

"I — I thought you'd left the door open when you went to work," I stammered. "I was going to close it."

Dad seemed to have trouble focusing on me. His eyes flickered and he passed his hand over them, then rubbed his head, making more spikes stick up. "Work? Yes-I-have-work-to-do.   Nothing-that-concerns-you." He pushed the garage door back open. "You-just-go-off-and-do-recreation-activities-with-your-friends."

He bared his teeth in a snarl that was maybe supposed to be a smile, then turned to go back inside.

As I scrambled to my feet, I got a look at what was littering up the workbench. Then I heard Frasier calling from the road and ran to get my bike.

"What were you doing?" asked Jessie when I met them at the road.

I explained about the noise I'd heard. "But it was only Dad. He's working on some stuff on the workbench."

Jessie's face screwed up in a puzzled scowl. "The workbench in the garage? Dad's never used that once since we moved here. He hates stuff like that," she said forcefully.

I nodded. I hadn't even told the strangest part. Taking a deep breath, I went on. "He's messing around with flashlights. He's got about a million of them in pieces all over the workbench," I told them. "More flashlights than we've ever owned in our lives."

"So he got a bargain on flashlights somewhere," said Frasier. "Big, hairy deal. Now let's go. We've already wasted half the morning."

We rode single file, in silence, until we reached the turnoff into the hills. As soon as we rolled our bikes onto the dirt path, I got a nasty feeling. Looking up at the shadowy hills, I said, "I think maybe this is a bad idea."

It felt like the hills were watching us eagerly, waiting for us to come closer. For some reason they reminded me of my dad in that strange shaggy coat, scraggly and menacing. The deep shadows between the hills were like huge mouths, ready to snap open and swallow us, leaving no trace. The way Mom and Dad were acting, they wouldn't even miss us.

"There's something out there," I said quietly. "I can feel it."

"Don't be a wuss," scoffed Frasier.

"No, he's right," Jessie insisted. "Something's watching us."

"Something?" asked Frasier, looking at Jessie with a grin. "Don't you mean some*one*?"

"You heard me right the first time," said Jessie, grim-faced.

"Uh-oh," said Frasier. "Sorry I asked." He jumped on his bike and started up the trail. "Come on, you dorks."

Jessie and I looked at each other. "What a jerk," said Jessie. "But we can't let him go up there alone."

"We're just spooking ourselves anyway," I said. "What could be out there?"

Jessie didn't answer. She just put her head down and got back on her bike. When we reached the foot of the three Harley Hills, Frasier was already climbing, pushing his bike into the burned area. Jessie and I followed, staying off the black earth. I couldn't shake a crawly feeling under my skin, but I told myself it was just my imagination working overtime.

We caught up to Frasier at the top of the hill where he was exploring the scorched star shape. "I think we should dig right here at the center where it looks like the lightning originally struck full force. Then we can see how far down the earth is charred," suggested Frasier.

"What good will that do?" asked Jessie.

Frasier shrugged and pulled his mother's gardening trowel out of his pack. He started to dig but the earth was so hard he could hardly chip it. Jessie climbed a little higher so she could look toward town. Watching her, I was surprised to see a grin light up her whole face.

"Hey, Nick. Come here!" she called.

I scrambled up beside her and looked out. There was our town, looking like a picture postcard with its houses all nestled in the trees and the tall church steeple rising into the sky.

"I wonder why we couldn't see it yesterday?" asked Jessie.

"Atmospheric inversion," I said, imitating Frasier. "Who knows?"

Jessie looked thoughtful. "It just shows there's a logical answer for everything," she said and then grinned at me. "Even midnight projects in the basement and peanut butter sandwiches for dinner and doughnuts for breakfast. Mom probably doesn't feel like cooking. Who can blame her?"

"Right," I said. "We ought to kick back and enjoy it while it lasts. They're probably working on some big surprise for us. We're just being silly, getting all bent out of shape because things are a little different at home."

Jessie laughed and started climbing up the rocks. "I'm going to go look for that eagle's nest," she said. "Give me a shout when Frase gets tired of his stupid digging."

I wandered away, staring aimlessly at the ground, wishing the sight of town had made everything better for me like it had for Jessie. But I still felt queasy, like something was biding its time, waiting.

Then suddenly I stopped, goosebumps crawling up my spine. There were weird footprints in the dust ahead of me.

And they weren't human footprints. They were like nothing I'd ever seen before. The toes fanned out for about a foot, each one as wide as a man's heel and the heel itself was a circle as big as a basketball. Whatever made these prints was huge! Maybe twelve feet tall. Taller. Maybe as tall as a tree.

"Frasier!" I shouted in a strangled voice. "Come here!"

Careful not to step on the prints, I followed them to see where they went. I didn't have to go far. The weird footprints ended at the edge of a cliff. Leaning over slowly, I looked down. The drop was sheer. Either this thing had suction cups on the bottom of its feet or it could fly.

I tried to imagine the beast that could have feet like this. The prints were not only as long as my arm and as wide as my whole body, they were deep. How could anything be that heavy, that tall, and still fly?

I knew one thing. There was nothing on earth that was even remotely like it.

I steadied myself against the rock wall. I felt weak just thinking about it. Fluttery inside.

But wait. I snatched my hand off the rock wall and the fluttery feeling stopped. Not really wanting to, I put my hand flat against the rock again, but lightly. There it was! The vibration. It was like the sound we'd heard — or felt — the night of the weird storm. A vibration in the rock.

There was something inside the hill.

My whole body started to tremble. I looked down at the huge, alien footsteps and how they ended at the edge of the cliff. Then I put my ear to the rock wall.

"EEEEEEEEEEEEEEEEEEEIIIIIIIIII!"

The high-pitched, ear-splitting noise was right in my ear. There was a sharp pain in my head and then the world went dark.

16

"Nick! Hey, Nick, are you okay?" Frasier's voice sounded distant, but his hand was shaking my arm.

My head throbbed and there was a sharp, hot pain in my temple. White spots danced in front of my eyes. And there was a frozen cold spot right in the center of my stomach.

"There's something — something inside the rock, burrowed in the hill," I said to Frasier, holding my head. "I heard it."

"Aw, man, I'm sorry," said Frasier. "That was me. I was just fooling around. I didn't expect you to jump like that."

I shook my head and winced at the pain. "No. I heard it."

"You mean this?" Frasier scrunched up his face and bared his teeth. "EEEEEEEEEEEEEEEEEEIIIIIII."

I stared at him.

"It was a goof," he said, backing away from me. "I saw you put your ear to the rock and I couldn't resist. It was supposed to be funny. But then you jumped and banged your head on that sharp bit sticking out — really, I'm sorry, Nick."

"For such a smart guy you're really a moron sometimes, you know that?" I said, feeling angry and foolish. But I was also relieved that it was just a jagged piece of rock I'd banged my head on and not an alien brain probe needle. "But it wasn't just you being a dork, Frase. I heard a vibration, like the night of the storm. Touch the rock. You can feel it."

He squinted at me, suspecting I had some kind of revenge in mind. But then he edged over to the rock and placed his hand against it. After a minute he shrugged. "I don't feel anything."

"What?" I put my hand on the rock wall, in the same place as before. Nothing. Nada. No flutters. No humming vibrations. Just warm rock. "It's gone now," I said, knowing he didn't believe me. "And look! What about these footprints? Don't tell me you can't see them."

Frasier shuffled his feet, embarrassed. "'Course I see them. I made them myself." He grinned. "Watch." He dug the ball of his foot into the ground, hard. Then he did it four more times, making five of the big toes. When he was done he stood on one foot and spun in a circle, making the heel that looked as wide and round as a basketball.

I was starting to get super irritated with him, plus, of course, feeling like a total idiot.

61

"I made them yesterday, for the visitors," explained Frasier. "I wanted the aliens to see them and think there was something majorly scarifying snooping around. I thought if they ended at the cliff the aliens would think it could fly, too." Frasier looked pleased with himself. "It was a dumbo move, I suppose. I mean, obviously there aren't any aliens. But the footprints look pretty real, don't they?"

I stomped over the prints, scuffing them out, and stalked past him. "I don't get you, Frasier. Yesterday you were all excited about UFOs and today it's like a big joke."

"Yesterday was yesterday," Frasier explained, hurrying after me. "I have a very active imagination. Everyone says so," he added proudly.

I shook my head in disgust, scanning the hillside for Jessie. She saw me and waved, starting down toward us. "I've had enough of this cheesy place," I announced. "I'm going home."

"No, wait," cried Frasier. "I brought lunch." He scurried past me and grabbed up his knapsack. "Look. Bologna, your favorite. And Oreos. Jessie won't want to miss out on Oreos."

I *was* kind of hungry. And if I insisted on leaving without lunch, Jessie would want to know why. It wouldn't be any fun explaining what an idiot I'd been, fooled by Frasier's goofy monster prints.

"Ooh, food," said Jessie, sliding down the last bit of

hill and landing beside us. "I didn't find the eagle nest, but I found a perfect place for a picnic. Come on."

Jessie led the way up. She clearly wasn't thinking about aliens or things watching us. But I kept looking over my shoulder as we climbed, feeling cold eyes drilling into my back. I told myself it was stupid, but I couldn't help it.

Jessie led us to a great spot. A broad, flat area along the side of the hill, it ended in a cliff with a long, sheer drop. We could look out over the whole badlands and down onto the town, too. Jutting out from the side of the hill over our heads was an overhang that provided plenty of shade.

There was only one thing wrong with this spot. It was right on top of the rock where I'd felt the vibrations. I sat down gingerly, expecting to feel the hum through the seat of my shorts.

But the ground felt ordinary, cool, and hard. Jessie reached for Frasier's knapsack, and soon the two of them were laughing and joking about UFO landings and rock-eating aliens with scorching fire for breath. I wished I could join in, but I couldn't — none of it seemed funny to me.

Frasier had brought a lot of sandwiches and we ate them all. Then we ate the whole package of cookies and washed it down with warm soda. So it was no wonder we were sleepy afterwards.

My eyelids got heavier and heavier. An uneasy

twinge in the back of my mind told me this wasn't a good time or place for a nap. I tried to sit up, to warn Frasier and Jessie that we should go, but my body felt so heavy, so sleepy. I heard Jessie begin to snore softly.

Then a hypnotic humming began to buzz inside my head. My eyes refused to open. My chin fell heavily onto my chest as if my jaw were made out of the same rock as these hills.

Zzzzzzz, Jessie snored.

I fell asleep and in my mind the hills began to grow eyes. Round eyes with no lids. They popped out of the rock on long stalks. The stalks swayed in the wind, then twisted to peer at us. Hundreds and hundreds of them sprouted from the rocks to stare at us.

I struggled to wake up from this terrible nightmare, but my body was pinned to the rock.

17

I stirred, dreaming that it was night and we'd been sleeping all afternoon. As I shifted, a rock dug into my hip and I woke up — to total blackness. It *was* night.

We'd been sleeping for hours and hours on this hard, rocky ground. How could that be? Unless — unless my dreams were true. I sat up, wincing from all the places sharp rocks had dug into me. Blurry images of dark dream shapes were fast fading, although I struggled to hold onto them.

What had happened to us? I remembered something about eyes and urgent whispering but that was all. It was scary to feel the dreams slipping away into the dark. Not knowing what had happened was worse than anything.

"Jessie! Frasier!" I called out. "Are you awake?" There was no moon and it was so dark I couldn't see anything but black shapes. I couldn't tell which were rocks and which were Jessie and Frasier.

Suddenly Jessie's voice came out of the dark. "Wow! What time is it?" I heard her move and saw her start to stand up, rubbing her leg. "Ow. I hurt all over. How could all three of us sleep so long on this cold rock?"

There was no sound from Frasier. "Frasier?" I called again. My voice sounded small and shaky. Nothing moved around us. No one answered. Where could he be? I called louder, *"FRASIER!"*

My shout echoed weakly between the hills and died away.

"Maybe they got him," whispered Jessie, sliding close to me. She sounded scared and close to crying. "The things in the hills."

"What do you mean?" I asked her, dreading the answer.

"It's what I dreamed," she whispered fearfully. "They crept down out of the hills. They were big and ugly and covered with scales. Tentacles stuck out all over them. They uncurled the tentacles and snatched us up, one by one."

"It was just a dream," I said. "A nightmare."

Just then, a cold, bony, scaly tentacle grabbed me by the ankle.

18

I thrashed to get free. I felt Jessie grab my arm to keep me from being carried away. The tentacle on my ankle wound its way around my leg.

As I opened my mouth to scream, another slimy tentacle, writhing with cold appendages, smacked down onto my face, covering my mouth and cutting off my air.

"Sssssssssss." There was a hissing sound in my ear. Was it sleeping gas? Was that how they'd got us before, kept us unconscious all day? With tremendous effort I twisted and felt one tentacle pull free of my face.

"Sssssshhhhhh! Be quiet." It was Frasier's voice!

"Frasier?" Was it really him? Or an alien mimicking his voice to fool us? As he let go of me, I realized the tentacles I had imagined were only Frasier's cold hands.

"Be quiet or they'll hear you," said Frasier. "If they haven't already with all that yelling."

It really was Frasier. I could see the outline of his big

head and the familiar gesture as he pushed his glasses up his nose. No alien could imitate that.

"Who? Who will hear us?" Jessie demanded urgently. "What did you see? Tell us!"

"You won't believe it!" Frasier exclaimed. There was a strange tone to his voice, as if he didn't know whether to be excited or scared. "It'll totally blow your mind! Come on, I'll show you. All you have to do is look over the edge of the cliff."

His hunched shape, keeping low to the ground, scuttled back in the direction of the cliff edge.

"Come on, guys, quick!" urged Frasier. "Before they get away."

I took a deep breath. "This better not be another stupid joke," I said quietly.

"I think he means it," Jessie said. Together we started after him, creeping carefully toward the edge.

As we moved we began to see a strange sort of bobbing, flickering light. Thin beams crossed and waved in the air.

I could see Jessie's face in the weird light. She looked scared. I figured I probably looked the same. Frasier was stretched out flat on his stomach, his head hanging over the edge.

"Get down!" he ordered, without looking back at us. "You don't want them to see you."

How could I feel so scared and curious at the same time? Jessie and I both dropped to the ground and crawled on our bellies toward the cliff edge. My breath sounded loud in the night quiet.

As our heads cleared the edge, we could suddenly see everything. The badlands stretched out below us, shadowy and secretive. And winding slowly through the narrow valley was a long line of people! Each person carried a flashlight. But the flashlights' beams were aimed up at the sky, not at the ground!

"There must be a hundred of them," said Frasier, handing Jessie his binoculars.

"Wow!" said Jessie breathlessly. "There's Mr. Rodriguez from the hardware store. And there's the school librarian, Mrs. Pringle. They're all from town!"

"Let me see!" I cried. But when Jessie handed me the binoculars, I almost wished she hadn't. It gave me a sinking feeling, seeing so many people we knew. There was Mrs. Perkins, who drove the school bus. Mr. Costello, the lawyer. And Mr. and Mrs. Grover, who lived down the street from us. I searched the line, afraid I was going to see our own parents, but I couldn't find them.

The people were all adults and they looked straight ahead. They didn't even speak to one another as they lurched and teetered along like a little kid's pull toy. The sight was so eerie I kept feeling if I blinked hard' enough it would disappear. But it didn't, no matter how hard I worked my eyes.

"They look like zombies," breathed Jessie.

She was right. The people moved stiffly and there was something wrong with their faces. The light beams crossed and bounced. But even when a bright light flashed directly into a person's eyes, there was no reaction. Their faces had absolutely no expression. It was like they were plastic dolls' faces. Only not cute. Not cute at all.

The line of staggering zombies reached the bottom of Harley Hill and started up. As they wound up between the crags and behind the rocks, we began to lose sight of them. But one thing was for sure. They were headed our way.

"What's going on?" Frasier asked, sounding truly stumped.

"Maybe they're looking for something," I suggested, feeling my mouth go dry.

"Yeah? What?" asked Frasier.

"Us."

19

There was a short silence as we watched the last of the bobbing flashlights disappear behind a rock face.

"I guess we better keep them in sight," Jessie suggested.

Feeling our way in the dark, we moved around the hill until we could see them again. The long line of people snaked along, weaving around boulders, coming up and up. Everybody's pace stayed exactly the same no matter how steep or flat or rocky the ground was.

They were coming closer. I recognized more and more people. There was the supermarket manager and the fire chief and Mrs. Stowe, who always made the best chocolate chip brownies for the school bake sale. But I didn't see my mom or dad. Or Frasier's parents either.

The adults plodded on, climbing the hill, their flashlights beamed into the sky. They could never catch us,

I realized. We could easily slip down the other side of the hill and they wouldn't even see us.

"I think I know where they're going," said Frasier.

"Me, too," said Jessie grimly.

I nodded in agreement and the three of us made our way down to where we'd stashed our bikes above the lightning strike. Quickly, we pushed them behind the big boulder and then crouched down to wait.

Waiting in the total darkness, the weirdness seemed even more terrifying. I had to clench my teeth to keep them from chattering.

But it wasn't long before we saw the beams weaving their way up to us. Footsteps crunched on the scorched rock.

Just as we suspected, they were heading for the arrow of burned earth that pointed the way to the top of Harley Hill. Without saying anything, the zombified grown-ups fanned out until they'd made a wide circle around the star points the lightning had blasted.

When the circle was complete, they all held their flashlights steady, aimed right up into the sky. Then they began to blink them on and off in unison.

"They're signaling!" cried Jessie in a hoarse whisper.

We watched in stunned silence for a while as the flashlights blinked. On. Off. On. Off.

"I learned Morse code in Boy Scouts," said Frasier, squinting as he concentrated. "But it's not Morse."

The adults weren't even looking up at the beams.

They just stared straight ahead at nothing. It was like they were just hollow shells of people. They just kept switching their lights on and off as if nothing else mattered.

Our eyes searched the sky but we saw nothing. No return flashes, no strange lightning, nothing but twinkling stars and blackness.

After a while the beams grew weaker. On, off, on, off. Dimmer and dimmer each time. Until finally the flashlights went dead. The circle of people just stood there for a moment, switching their dead lights. Somehow that made it worse — that they kept going when there was no light left. But at last their hands went limp and the flashlights fell to the ground.

The circle began to waver and break up. People shifted from foot to foot. They didn't seem to know what they were doing or what to do next.

"It's like they're sleepwalking," said Jessie.

"I guess," I agreed, shifting uncomfortably in my hiding spot. "But what can we do about it?"

Jessie looked at me, then at Frasier, her eyes gleaming. "Wake them up!" she whispered fiercely.

20

Jessie grabbed her bicycle and stood astride it. She looked over her shoulder at us. "You guys all set?"

"Ready to rock and roll," Frasier answered, tightening the strap on his bike helmet.

"On the count of three," I said, glad we were finally *doing* something. I refused to think about whether it would work or not. Or whether whatever happened to the adults might happen to us, too. "One, two, THREE!"

We zoomed out from behind the boulder and raced down the hill, straight for the line of zombified adults. The balloons on Frasier's tires whomped as we sped and skidded over the rocks and dirt.

"*AAAAAAAIIIIIIIEEEEEEEEE!*" we screamed at the top of our lungs, careening down the hill. "*YAAAAAAAAAA-HOOOOOOOOOO!*"

But nothing happened. They didn't seem to hear us,

even though our voices split the night and shattered the quiet. They weren't going to move.

Then I had a brainstorm. I hoped it would work. "Hey, Mr. Grover! Mr. Rodriguez! Watch out!"

As I'd hoped, the two men's heads snapped around when they heard their names. Their eyes blinked. They saw the bicycles hurtling toward them and jumped out of the way.

We all started yelling out names and more people snapped out of their trances, blinking and looking around them in confusion. "What are you doing here?" they asked each other. "What am I doing here?"

We drove our bikes into their midst and pulled on people's sleeves, yelling their names into their faces. "How did we get here?" they asked, slow and confused.

I jumped onto a rock and began to tell them what we'd seen — all about them following each other single file and the flashlight signaling. But none of them seemed to remember any of it. "It must be some kind of atmospheric thing," said Mr. Forester, the fire chief. "Something in the air that induced mass sleepwalking."

"Yeah," said Frasier under his breath. "Right."

Some of the people turned and began to straggle down the hill. Others followed until the whole crowd of people was moving. But they didn't seem to know what to do. They wandered off the path, stumbling over rocks and into holes. When the first ones reached the bottom, they turned the wrong way, away from town.

"Whoa," cried Jessie, pushing off on her bike. "This way. Follow us."

We rode after stragglers and got them pointed in the right direction. Most of the people still moved like sleepwalkers, as if they weren't really sure how arms and legs were supposed to work. But finally we got them all to the bottom of Harley Hill and headed back to town.

"It's like herding cattle," muttered Jessie as we joined up again.

"I'll ride behind and make sure we don't lose any," said Frasier.

It took a while but eventually everyone was on the road to town. Soon lights and houses began to appear. The crowd thinned out a little as people dropped off to go to their own homes.

"Oh, no. Look!" said Jessie, pointing down the road ahead of us.

Approaching us were two bobbing flashlights. "Not more of them," she groaned. "Is this going to go on all night?"

"No," I said with determination. "We're going to wake them up right now." I stood on the pedals and put on a burst of speed.

"*AAAAAAAAAIIIIIIIIIEEEEEEEE!,*" I screamed, heading full speed straight for them.

Jessie was right behind me, her yell piercing the night.

But suddenly I squeezed the brakes hard, skidding across the pavement. "Mom! Dad!"

21

Glaring light hit my eyes and blinded me. I felt the bike skid and knew I was going to fall. I couldn't see a thing.

Then all of a sudden a giant hand snatched my bike off the ground. The bike stopped abruptly in midair. I stuck my feet out but couldn't find the pavement. All I could feel was empty air.

The next second the light fell away from my eyes and I saw it was only the flashlight in Dad's hand. My foot struck the pavement as Dad's other hand steadied my bike.

His eyes were dark pools in his expressionless face.

Jessie pulled up beside me. "Mom," she cried. "What's happening to everybody?"

"Everybody? Let's-talk-about-what-you've-been-up-to-young-lady," Dad said. "And-you-young-man. What-are-you-doing-screaming-around-on-your-bike-late-at-night?" The words sounded like the sort of thing Dad might say but the tone was all wrong. He sounded like an actor pretending to be stern.

The sound of that voice filled me with cold dread.

"The-two-of-you-had-us-worried-half-to —" Dad frowned and looked at Mom. "What's-the-word? Mortality?"

"Death," Mom said, her eyes hard and blank. "Worried-half-to-death. When-we-realized-you-and-Jessie weren't-in-your-rooms, we-came-out-looking-for-you."

Dad nodded as if pleased with Mom's explanation. But he seemed to have lost interest in us. He was searching the eyes of the other adults as if he were looking for something he couldn't find.

Jessie explained that we'd fallen asleep in the afternoon and woke to find the hills full of sleepwalking adults. "We had to help them find their way back to town," she said.

"A-likely-story," said Mom as if reading lines in a foreign language.

"It's true. You can ask them," I said, spinning around to find one of the people we'd helped. But the streets were almost empty. Most of the adults had melted away, gone back to their homes. Then, across the street I caught sight of one. "There," I told Dad. "Ask Mr. Rodriguez. He was there."

"'Evening, Gus," Dad said, waving to Mr. Rodriguez

and baring his teeth in a meaningless grimace. "Some kind-of-do-up-at-the-Hills-tonight? My-boy-says-he-saw-a-lot-of-people-climbing-Harley-Hill."

Mr. Rodriguez looked blank. "Not-that-I-know about," he said flatly. "There's-a-lot-of-folks-out-and-about-tonight-though. Seems-like-everyone-had-the-same-idea-I-did — it's-a-real-nice-night-for-a-walk."

Jessie and I exchanged glances. Mr. and Mrs. Grover walked by and waved. "Hi-Bert. Hi-Amy. Lovely-night-for-a-stroll-isn't-it?"

There was no expression in any of their voices. They were just going through the motions of acting normal.

Dad faced us. "We-must-deal-with-this-unusual-situ-ation," he said. "Your-behavior-is-unacceptable. I-think-we-need-a-few-changes-around-here."

"What kind of changes?" asked Jessie, her voice squeaking a little.

Mom and Dad were both silent a moment, although they didn't look at each other. Then they spoke in unison. "Grounded," they said grimly. "You're-both-grounded."

"For how long?" I cried, seeing my summer begin to shrink.

"Until-you-start-acting-normal-again," said Dad.

Mom nodded. "Perfectly-normal," she said.

22

It was almost a relief to be grounded, I told myself the next morning, after Jessie and I once more fended for ourselves at breakfast. Mom and Dad were both in the basement again.

We listened at the door but couldn't make out what they were doing. All we could hear was things being dragged over the floor and the occasional murmur of voices.

But at least today we wouldn't have to go back to Harley Hills.

A couple of Jessie's friends came by — girls from school — but I didn't hang around. I went back up to my room.

But what was there to do? I didn't feel like starting a new model airplane or reading a book — not on a sunny summer morning. Those things were for rainy days. I was staring aimlessly out the window, worrying as usual, when my door banged open.

I jumped at least a foot, but it was only Jessie. "There is such a thing as knocking," I said, embarrassed.

"The door wasn't all the way closed," said Jessie, plopping down to sit cross-legged on the floor. "Notice anything strange around here this morning?"

I shrugged. What wasn't strange these days? But I didn't say that. "Okay, what?" I said.

"For starters Mom and Dad said they came to look for us when we weren't in our rooms, right? Well, how come they didn't notice that we didn't show up for dinner?"

"Mom hasn't been into meals much lately," I said. It sounded kind of lame, even to me.

"Yeah, I noticed," said Jessie. "But if you don't think that's weird, then how about the fact that Dad hasn't gone to work since the night of the storm? And he's not on vacation."

"So maybe he's taking some time off. He's done that before," I argued halfheartedly.

Jessie shook her head. "This is different. None of the other adults are going to work either. Ashley and Judy noticed it," said Jessie, referring to her school friends. "And Frasier told me his parents are staying home, too. They all said their parents are just hanging around the house. Like they're waiting for something to happen."

"Like what? An invasion?" I asked sarcastically.

But Jessie didn't scoff or roll her eyes like I expected.

"I don't know," she said, frowning. "That's what scares me."

Suddenly something clattered against the house. We stared at each other, startled.

SCREEEEEEEEEEEEEEECH!

Both of us jumped. Jessie gasped and pointed at the window, her mouth working soundlessly.

A pale, white hand was clawing desperately at the glass, trying to break through.

13

Maybe it wasn't the smartest thing to do but I leaped up and ran to the window.

Scriiitch. Screeeeeeeeeech.

The writhing hand scrabbled and clawed at the glass, making an awful noise. I threw open the window, furious and terrified, ready to launch myself at the alien. But as I leaned out the cold fingers fastened on my wrist with an iron grip.

It started to pull me out the window. Jessie grabbed my waist and pulled the other way. My arm felt like it was coming out of its socket.

"Nick," came a strained, raspy voice. "Let me in."

"Frasier?" Jessie let go of me and I almost tumbled out the window.

"Yeah, it's me," said Frasier, gripping the windowsill with one hand and my arm with the other. "Help me up."

I should have known. Frasier and his tricks!

"Why didn't you use the front door?" I demanded as Jessie and I heaved Frazier into the room. He had a skinned knee, and there were bits of dirt and leaves sticking out of his crew cut.

"Couldn't," he said, shaking his head and scattering leaf bits all over the floor. "I'm grounded, too, remember? Since your parents brought me home last night. *My* parents hadn't even noticed I was missing until then. Anyway, my mom thinks I'm cleaning my room."

Jessie leaned forward and plucked a twig off of Frasier's shoulder. "Are your parents acting strange, Frasier?"

Frasier laughed. He took off his glasses and wiped them on his shirt. "My parents are always acting weird. So I can't really tell if they're any weirder than usual. But, hey, I'm more worried about the squirrels than I am about the humans. Not to mention the birds."

"Squirrels? Birds?" I echoed. "What are you talking about?"

Frasier beamed, looking pleased that he knew something we didn't. "Come on. I'll show you."

Jessie shot me a warning look, like she thought it was Frasier that was squirrelly. "We're grounded, Frase, remember? I don't want to get in any more trouble."

"You've got to see this," Frasier insisted. "It's truly bizarre."

He started for the window but I stopped him. "We'll go out the kitchen door," I said. "Then, if my mom catches us, we can say we were getting something to eat."

The three of us moved very quietly down the stairs. There wasn't a sound in the house. It felt deserted. But my heart pounded. I kept expecting Mom or Dad to be hiding behind a door, ready to leap out, yelling "Gotcha!" as we snuck past.

We crept down the hall and nothing happened. The kitchen was so clean it looked like no one ever ate there. Mom liked to hum or sing while she worked but when I put my ear to the basement door I didn't hear so much as a peep.

The silent house gave me a creepy feeling. I felt like our parents had moved out and left us.

Frasier opened the kitchen door. "Ready? Let's go."

We slipped out and headed across the lawn toward the woods at the back end of our yard. I kept expecting someone to stop us, but no one did.

The sun was hot, but as soon as we stepped into the woods, cool air surrounded us. It was quiet here, too. Too quiet. Usually there were birds flitting around even in the middle of the day, and squirrels chattered at everything that went by. But except for a little breeze ruffling the leaves above us, there wasn't a sound.

"Look," said Frasier in an awed hush, pointing up into the trees.

I looked up. Rows and rows of glowing eyes were staring at us.

24

Jessie gasped. It sounded loud in the silence. The eyes seemed to hang in the cool darkness, glowing red, yellow, green, like tiny Christmas tree lights. Hundreds of glowing eyes. All watching us.

I wanted to flee but I was afraid to move. My eyes adjusted slowly to the dimness after the bright sun. After a few minutes I could see that the eyes belonged to squirrels.

They lined the branches of every tree around us. The squirrels were packed together as tight as sardines in a can. There were squirrels in every nook and cranny of every tree. They just sat there tensed on their haunches, perfectly still, staring at us with those weird, glowing eyes.

Jessie moved closer to me. I could feel her trembling. "Squirrels are supposed to run around," she whispered. "Whenever I come out here they chatter at me like crazy. But these squirrels act like they're hypnotized or something."

"I've never seen so many in one place before," breathed Frasier.

"It's like they've come here from all over," I said. "I want to get closer. See if they'll run away or if they're paralyzed or what."

Frasier nodded. All three of us crowded together, approaching very slowly. The eyes seemed to glow hotter, the closer we got.

"What's that noise?" whispered Jessie.

It sounded like the revving of a motor a long way off. But as soon as Jessie spoke I realized it wasn't a motor and it wasn't far off. The woods were no longer silent.

"Uh-oh," said Frasier.

"Grrrrrrrrrrrrrrrrrrrrrrrrrrrrrr!"

The squirrels were growling. The sound came from deep in their chests. It was growing louder, more menacing. Was it my imagination or were the squirrels tensing to spring?

"GRRRRRRRRRRRRRRRRRRRRRR!"

"I don't know about this," I said nervously. "Maybe we should leave."

Jessie and Frasier nodded but none of us moved a muscle. We were afraid to turn our backs on the squirrels. "Maybe they're rabid," said Frasier. "Raccoons get rabies, right? Why not squirrels?"

"Sure," said Jessie sarcastically. "All the squirrels in the woods get rabies at exactly the same time. Get real."

Suddenly a noisy gust of wind sprang up. It came from every direction at once, ruffling our hair, tugging at our clothes. Whirlwinds of leaves rose off the forest floor and smacked our faces, snagging in our clothes and hair.

"We better get out of here," cried Jessie. "It must be another storm coming up."

We turned to run. But we didn't get far. No more than a step.

"*GAK!*" yelled Jessie.

I felt my heart stop.

It wasn't a storm that created the sudden wind. It was the wings of birds! Our path was blocked by a solid wall of fluttering birds! Hundreds of them had landed on the ground right behind us. Even as we stared, more arrived. The ground was a writhing mass of black and brown feathers.

My throat felt thick. "What do we do?" I asked.

As if in answer to my question, the birds began to caw and shrill and shriek at us threateningly, their beady eyes hard and cold.

"*CAAAW! WWRREEEEEEP! SHREEEEEEEEEE!*"

The noise was deafening. Jessie clapped her hands to her ears. I gritted my teeth to try and stop them chattering from fear.

I felt an elbow in my ribs. "This way," shouted Frasier.

I could barely hear him over the angry, awful din of birds. I nodded and pulled at Jessie. But as we started to plunge into the bushes, the whole flock rose like a black cloud and shifted to block our way.

"What do they want?" Jessie cried fearfully.

"I think they want *us*," I shouted back.

The birds kept their eyes on us, watching for any attempt to escape.

25

We huddled together, trembling in fear. "We've got to get out of here," I said.

Suddenly there was a huge roar of wings as loud as a jet engine. The mass of birds rose off the ground. Were they leaving?

Wings beat the air as they hovered, and leaves and bits of dirt filled our eyes.

"I can't see!" cried Frasier, ripping off his glasses to claw the dirt out of his eyes.

The hovering birds pointed their beaks at us. They were going to dive-bomb us. Peck us to pieces!

We didn't stand a chance, three kids against a thousand crazed birds. Suddenly one of them rose higher, folded its wings, and dove straight at Frasier. He was still rubbing his eyes and didn't see it.

I grabbed his arm and yanked him out of the way. All the birds began to shriek and caw. They were coming after us. "Run!" I shouted, dragging Frasier by the arm.

"*CAAAAAW! SSHHRRRRRRRRREEEEEEEP! CAW! CAW!*"

The three of us plunged into the bushes as the birds dove at our heads, screaming in our ears. We ran as hard as we could, but the undergrowth slowed us down. Thorns ripped at our clothes and roots snagged at our feet.

The birds fluttered maniacally around our heads. "*CAAW, CAAAW, CAAAAWWWWWWWWWWW!*"

Ducking away from their sharp beaks, we could hardly see where we were going. Frasier ran into a tree and fell down, stirring the birds to a gleeful frenzy. Jessie helped him up and pushed him forward while I found a stick and brandished it at the attacking birds.

They flew higher, just out of reach, and seemed to laugh at our puny efforts to save ourselves. "*KAKAKA-KAKAKAKAKA!*"

"Come on," yelled Jessie. I dropped the stick and followed, trying to run and cover my head at the same time. I never knew the brush of bird's wings could feel so terrifying.

Then a robin darted over my head and attacked Jessie, snatching at her hair with its beak and claws.

"*EEEEEEEEEEEEEEEEEIIIIIIII,*" screamed Jessie, shaking her head wildly and batting at the bird. The robin tangled its feet in her hair, plucking out strands with its beak, its wings flicking like some maddened bat.

I smacked my hand at the bird. It let go of Jessie's hair

and fluttered up out of my reach, making a piercing, warlike noise. The birds swirled around our heads as I pulled Jessie along.

I caught a glimpse of bright sun through the thick woods, and my heart lifted. "The road," I shouted. "This way!"

But hope faded fast. Would the flock of crazed birds follow us out of the woods? Their noise was even louder now and they dove repeatedly at our hair, pulling strands with painful little yanks.

We crashed through the bushes at the side of the road and emerged into the sunlight, panting and whimpering.

And suddenly there was silence.

The attack stopped as abruptly as it had started. Out of the woods, we were safe. At least for now.

Frasier, breathing hard, wiped his forehead. His glasses were crooked and leaves and feathers were stuck in his bristly crew cut. Jessie's hair was a huge tangle, like a bird's nest. I brushed my head and watched small black and gray feathers flutter to the road.

"This is ridiculous," Frasier grumbled. "Now even the sparrows are trying to kill us."

Jessie's eyes looked very big and dark in her ghost-white face. "Nick, you know how every spring I save all the hair from my hairbrush and every morning I put it out in the forsythia bush for the birds to make their nests?"

I nodded.

"Well, I don't think I'm going to do that anymore," she said and started trudging for home. She wasn't going very fast, but Frasier and I were so exhausted we still had to struggle to catch up with her.

None of us had much to say, but I knew Jessie was thinking the same thing I was. Maybe Mom and Dad had a good reason for grounding us. Something didn't want us messing around outside, and our parents just might know what it was.

The thought made me shudder. Did the big project in the basement have something to do with what was happening to the birds and squirrels? Were our parents responsible?

Jessie and I crept back into the house as quietly as we could. But it didn't matter. There was so much noise coming from the basement, Mom and Dad wouldn't have heard us if we'd shouted we were home.

SCCCCCCCCCRRRRRRRRRRRRAAAAAAAPPPPE!
BAANG!

It sounded like something metal and very heavy was being dragged and pushed across the floor. There were grunting noises that didn't sound like either of our parents.

We glanced at each other and bolted for the stairs, not stopping until we were outside Jessie's room. "I'm really scared," said Jessie. Even with dirt all over her face, I could see dark circles under her eyes. "We have to do something."

94

I nodded. "But what? Whatever is causing this is stronger than our parents."

"Yes," Jessie agreed, wincing. "But for some reason it doesn't affect us. That has to count for something."

"You're right. Maybe it doesn't have any power over kids," I said. "Tell you what. Let's each go to our rooms and think hard about a plan. We'll meet at your room in an hour and see what we've got."

"Good idea," said Jessie enthusiastically. "We'll think of something."

But half an hour later I was still sitting at my desk, chewing the end of my pen. Everything I could think of led to just one thing. We had to go back to Harley Hills. That's where it had started, and I was absolutely certain that whatever evil thing was doing all this was in those hills somewhere.

But every time I thought about going, I started to shake.

So naturally my heart slammed against my ribs when I heard sneaky footsteps in the hall outside my door.

"Who's there?" I demanded, the challenging tone ruined by a squeak in the middle.

"Me." It was Jessie. She pushed open the door and slipped in. Her face was pasty white and her eyes were big and scared.

I leaped up from the bed in alarm. "Jessie! What is it? What's the matter now?"

Jessie shuddered and pointed toward the window. Her mouth worked but she couldn't get any words out. "L-l-look," she finally stuttered. "Look out the w-w-window."

I ran to the window and looked out. And the hair rose up on the back of my neck.

26

People — adults — were coming out of all the houses I could see. They lurched out their doors, moving jerkily and leaving the doors swinging wide behind them. Moving like sleepwalkers. Or zombies.

"Do you see?" breathed Jessie.

"I see them," I said, craning my neck and looking out through the backyards. As I watched, all the people disappeared around the sides of their houses, heading for the street.

"It's worse from my room," moaned Jessie.

"Let's check it out," I said, grabbing her hand. Jessie's room was next to mine, but there was a better view of the street. I gasped when I looked down.

All up and down the street, doors were swinging wide and people were staggering into the road. Their jaws hung slack and they stared blindly ahead of them.

Mr. Mason walked into Mr. Forester and the two of them bounced off each other like rubber. They wobbled like toy tops, then got themselves upright again and went on with the crowd, never saying a word to each other.

"Ow," I said as Mrs. Pringle walked smack into a tree. But her expression didn't change. She backed up a few steps and veered off in a slightly different direction, like one of those kid's windup cars that bumps into things and buzzes off again.

The people looked rubbery and stiff at the same time. They bounced off each other. They bumped into parked cars and trees like they didn't see them. Just like those battery toys, they would back up and start going again, all of them heading in the same direction — north, out of town. But their arms and legs were jerky, as if they had strings attached like puppets.

"They're heading for Harley Hills," I said bleakly.

"Oh, no," cried Jessie. "Look!"

But I'd already seen. Mom and Dad came lurching out of the house, their legs jerking in unison. They joined the crowd and disappeared into it. "We've got to save them!" I shouted, heading for the door, Jessie on my heels.

As we pounded down the stairs, I began to feel a faint vibration from under the floor. It seemed to rise from deep in the ground, up through the foundation of the house and the soles of my feet. It made my bones rattle and my skin buzz. I clenched my teeth to keep them from chattering.

We dashed out through the open door.

"Yaaagllub," yelled Jessie, like the wind had been knocked out of her.

I turned to see what was wrong and — wham! — Mr. Harper, who weighed about 300 pounds, walked into me, knocking me instantly to the ground. He kept going as if he didn't notice.

All I could see around me were churning, jerking legs. "Hey," I called out, trying to scramble to my feet. A foot caught me in the ribs and I went down again. Where was Jessie?

A jolt of fear went through me as I thought of us being trampled by our own neighbors. I wriggled along the ground trying to get out of their path. But mobs of people were careening across our front yard. They were everywhere.

I rolled into a ball to try and protect myself. "Jessie, where are you?" I called out. No answer. Then a foot planted itself in my side. "Aaaaaaah!" I twisted and the foot slid off. It was Mr. Rodriguez. He teetered as if he were going to fall on me.

"Mr. Rodriguez," I yelled. "Wake up!"

He recovered his balance and backed away but never looked at me, never changed his shuffling, lurching gait.

A hand gripped my shoulder and tried to haul me up. It was Jessie. Somehow she'd gotten to her feet. "Come on, Nick!" she yelled. "We've got to hurry."

It felt weird to be shoving at adults, but the crowd was so thick it was the only way I could get back on my feet. As soon as I shoved, they wobbled and stopped, then turned and went around me. Their eyes never once focused on anything.

"Mrs. Pringle! Mr. Forester! Mr. Mason!"

We tried yelling their names like we had the other night, but they didn't respond. They didn't even blink. My stomach shriveled to a cold, hard ball of dread.

"I can't see Mom and Dad," said Jessie, jumping to try and see over the heads of all the people. But it was no use. Mom and Dad were completely swallowed up by the crowd. And the crowd was pressing on us more thickly every minute. If we didn't get out of here soon, we'd be swept along.

"Let's get our bikes," I yelled to Jessie, who was already getting separated from me.

She nodded. "We'll head them off."

27

The sun was sinking rapidly. Strange clouds were boiling up along the horizon over Harley Hills, casting an eerie glow.

Jessie and I grabbed our bikes and started pedaling furiously up the road. We had to get ahead of them, figure out a way to stop them somehow. Maybe Mom and Dad would recognize our desperate voices and wake up. Then they could help us wake the others.

But people kept stumbling into our path. Then we'd have to brake hard to keep from hitting them. Most of the time, we no sooner got back on our bikes than somebody else would stagger into us.

"This is no good," said Jessie. "We're not even moving as fast as they are."

I nodded, swallowing hard. "There's only one thing to do," I said.

Jessie nodded back, looking scared and serious.

"We'll have to go through the woods," she said, her voice small.

"It's shorter, at least," I said, veering over to a path I knew. I tried to keep my voice steady as I looked into the blackness of the woods, but I was shaking all over.

"What about the birds and squirrels?" asked Jessie.

I bit my lip and hopped back on the bike. "Just pedal fast and keep your head down," I said.

The woods were dark, but the sky was glowing brighter now and there was just enough light to see the narrow path. The vibration in the earth seemed stronger, too. "Can you feel that?" I asked my sister.

"The humming?" Jessie responded grimly. "I can feel it coming up from the ground. Right up through my tires. It reminds me of the pipe organ at church. The lowest note. You can barely hear it, but it makes the furniture shake."

I just grunted. That was exactly what I'd thought the night of the storm. I tried to push that memory out of my mind. We had work to do. I kept my head lowered and my eyes on the rutted path through the trees.

But we hadn't gone far when I heard a squeak from Jessie. Reluctantly I looked up. Eyes glowed from the tree branches. Thousands and thousands of tiny red, yellow, and green eyes, all of them fixed on us.

My insides seemed to liquefy. I wanted to drop the bike right there and hightail it back to our house. But I couldn't do that. We had to save our parents. So I put my head down and pedaled harder.

Zoom! Swish! Out of the darkness I felt the flutter of birds' wings close to my face. I flinched and almost fell but steadied myself and kept going. The birds flapped closer, brushing my skin with their whispery wings. I gritted my teeth and gripped the handlebars, wishing I could close my eyes.

"Behind us!" yelled Jessie, her voice cracking and shrill.

I risked a glance over my shoulder. A big, dark shape slipped in and out of the trees, chasing down the path after us. I only got a glimpse before I had to look forward again to keep from crashing into a tree.

But one look was enough to send my pulse racing. It looked like the hugest bird I had ever seen, its big wings flapping into tree trunks and branches.

"Faster," I shouted as a crow swooped down inches from my nose.

I batted at the bird and looked behind us again. The flapping thing raced along after us. It was gaining. And it no longer looked like a bird at all. It was too bulky, and what I had thought were wings looked like a long cape whipping out behind the thing.

But it was definitely flying. My heart was pumping like mad, but my blood ran cold.

I risked another glance back.

The thing was gaining on us. Getting closer and closer.

My bike wobbled dangerously as panic shot through me. I whipped around and got control of my bike just as the front wheel hit a big rock and bounced high into the air. I shuddered to think what might have happened if I'd hit the rock when I wasn't looking.

"Faster!" I shouted to Jessie.

We had to outdistance the caped monster. I stepped harder on the pedals, bouncing over ruts, feeling the shock go right through me.

"Ah-heeeeeeeeeeeeeeeeeeeeeee!"

A bloodcurdling scream erupted from the darkness.

28

The thing had got Jessie! For one long instant my heart seemed to stop completely. I tromped on the brakes and at that same instant two things happened.

First, I heard Jessie's voice right behind me. "What was that?" she called out shakily. "It sounded like a person."

And the second thing was another scream. "Help," it yelled. "Help me!"

Jessie and I looked at each other in horror. "Frasier!" we exclaimed together.

Both of us rammed our bikes around on the path and sped back toward the sound of Frasier's cry, ducking our heads against the slap of birds' wings. "That thing must have got him!" Jessie called over her shoulder.

Frasier was thrashing around on the ground, wrestling with the caped figure. We dumped our bikes and ran to help. Jessie and I both broke small branches off a tree as we ran and aimed them like spears at the shadowy thing on the ground attacking our friend.

"Hu-*YAAAAAAAAAAAAAAAAA!*" we screamed, startling two grackles, which burst into the air, complaining raucously.

The shadow thing sprang up after them, shaking its fist at the birds, its cape flapping as it jumped in rage, growling. We flinched away, scanning the ground frantically. Where was Frasier?

"Thanks, guys." Frasier's voice came out of the caped monster. "Those birds almost had my eyes pecked out."

"Frasier?" I stared in amazement. "Is that you?"

Jessie was already examining his face, wiping off the blood from a nasty scratch with a tissue.

"Those birds aimed straight at my eyes," he complained, his voice shaking. "Knocked me right off my bike."

I moved closer, frowning at his cape. He had on the Superboy cape from his Halloween costume! That's the "monster" we'd seen. Frasier shrugged sheepishly. "I thought I'd protect myself with this old cape," he said. "Keep the birds off. But it didn't work."

"Sure, Frase, sure," I said. The birds were regrouping, getting ready to swarm over us again. "Come on. Let's get going."

"You heading the same way?" Jessie asked our friend, ducking a starling and slapping at a blue jay.

"The badlands," said Frasier, still breathing in little gasps. He shuddered. "Something is calling all the adults to Harley Hills."

We got back on our bikes, trying to ignore the shrill screaming of the birds and the beady, glowing stares of the squirrels. We kept our heads down and didn't speak as we pedaled the rest of the way through the woods.

Just before we reached the edge of the woods, the birds gathered in a swirling cloud for one big attack. They darted and raced around our heads, cawing and shrieking.

"CAAAAWWW! RRRRAAAAAWWWW!"

Frasier tried to hide under his cape and his bike skidded dangerously, narrowly missing a tree. Jessie almost rammed into him, and I braked hard to avoid her, then almost fell when a bird landed on my head.

"KAKAKAKAKAKAKAKA!" shrilled the birds gleefully as the bikes wobbled and lurched.

"Just keep your heads down and *GO!*" I yelled.

I saw what I thought were nods from the others, and then we were hunched grimly over the handlebars, pedaling furiously, doing our best to ignore the slap and whisper of prickly feathers.

We burst out of the trees and suddenly, just like before, the birds left us alone.

We turned onto the path through the badlands. The horizon glowed ominously under boiling clouds, but we saw no sign of the adults.

"Let's head up that hill," Jessie suggested. "Maybe from the top we can see which way they went."

It was more of a gentle rise than a hill but it was

enough. From the top, we could see a snaking line of eerily silent grown-ups. They were shuffling and lurching their way toward the Harley Hills and whatever was glowing on the horizon. Some of the grown-ups carried flashlights which they didn't aim at anything, some just stumbled along in the dark.

"They don't even look human," said Frasier fearfully. "They look like windup toys."

"We've got to try and wake them," said Jessie, her knuckles white where she was gripping the handlebars of her bike.

"Last time we snapped them out of it by making a lot of noise," Frasier pointed out.

Jessie and I exchanged troubled glances. "We tried that earlier, when we left our house," I said. "It didn't work this time."

"But we have to try again," Jessie insisted. "We have to do *something*. And maybe here in the hills it will work, just like it did before."

"All right," I said, not having any other plan to offer. "It's worth a try."

We positioned our bikes at the top of the ridge. "Ready?" asked Jessie. "Count of three. One, two, *THREE!*"

We tore off down the hill, feeling the wind whistling past our ears, screaming at the top of our lungs.

"*YYAAAAAAAAIIIIIIIIIIIEEEEEEEEEEE!*"

The light in the far sky pulsed brighter, like sheet

lightning. Something was out there. Something that wasn't human. Could it see us? Did it know who we were?

The feeling that maybe it did hit me like an icy fist in the gut.

29

Screaming like banshees, we reached the line of adults, but none of them flinched or turned in our direction. They just kept marching along at the same jerking, sleepwalker's pace.

We yelled louder and called out their names as we wove our bikes through the line. But there was no reaction. Our eardrums were aching from our own noise, but these people never even noticed. It was beyond weird, as if we were invisible.

The townspeople staggered on, toward the hills and the glowing light.

Frustrated, angry, and scared, I picked out gray-haired Mrs. Pringle, our nice school librarian, and put my face right into hers. *"Mrs. Pringle!"* I screamed at the top of my lungs. "Wake up! Right now!"

Her eyebrows twitched. I was so startled, I almost fell off my bike.

"Wow, I think she maybe heard you," cried Jessie excitedly. "Let's try again." She picked out Mr. Forester, the fire chief, and began to scream his name right in his ear. Frasier did the same to Mr. Wilcox, and I tried again with Mrs. Pringle.

"Mrs. Pringle," I shouted in her ear. "Are you there? Can you hear me?"

This time her whole head turned toward me. My heart soared. We were going to win! We were going to wake up the adults and keep them from walking into the light! "Mrs. Pringle," I yelled joyfully.

Her mouth opened and out came a deep, gruff voice. "Follow-meeee," it said, with as much expression as a robot. "Follow-meeee."

Mrs. Pringle had never had a voice like that in her life. Her eyes were on my face but they didn't see me. Those eyes were flat and dead. They didn't see anything.

Slowly her hands floated up from her sides like they didn't belong to her. Her fingers jerked and spasmed. "Follow-meee."

Those bony old hands were reaching for me.

I jerked back in shock and nearly fell off my bike. Mrs. Pringle kept coming. Her outstretched hands clutched at me, her fingers straining to get me. Twisting to get away, I lost my balance. My foot got tangled in the spokes of my bike and all I could see was those fingers twitching as they neared. I tried desperately not to fall.

Ignoring the pain in my mashed toes, I yanked my foot free of the bike spokes. "Mrs. Pringle, wake up!" I pleaded as I ducked away from those clawlike fingers.

Mrs. Pringle hissed as her fingers raked the air, right where my head had been a second before. We had to get out of here. Our plan to wake the adults was not working.

I started to hop on the bike but something tugged at the bottom of my jeans. I looked down. My pant leg was caught in the chain!

"Follow-meeee!" chanted Mrs. Pringle in her flat bass voice. I was certain I heard a note of gleeful triumph.

I jerked at my leg but it wouldn't come free of the chain. And then I felt Mrs. Pringle's fingers fasten on my T-shirt and curl around the material.

She had me. *It* had me. For an instant I froze as a bolt of terror flooded through my body. What if I turned into a sleepwalking zombie like Mrs. Pringle?

I was so limp with fear my knees were knocking together and buckling.

"Help!" I yelled, thrashing around to get free. Where were Frasier and Jessie? Why didn't they help?

With my pant leg stuck in the chain, I couldn't let go of the bike to fight off Mrs. Pringle. The bike was a heavy weight attached to my ankle. If I let go, it would drag me to the ground.

Holding the handlebars with one hand, trying to

keep the bike upright, I grabbed at the old lady's wrist with my other hand and pulled.

Amazingly, her grip loosened on my shirt instantly. There was no strength in that zombielike hand. But her other hand fastened on my wrist. Her flat eyes seemed to gleam in the darkness. "Come-to-the-light," she said in that strange voice. "Follow-meeee. Follow-usssss."

"No!" I screamed, jerking my arm out of her weak grasp. I stumbled, dragging the bike, and felt her fingers twist in the fabric of my shirt once more.

Then a heavier, stronger hand fell on my shoulder. There was a grunt, and I felt myself ripped out of Mrs. Pringle's grasp. The glow on the horizon shone right in my eyes.

This is it, I thought, distantly feeling my bike fall away from me. I'm being taken to the light.

30

"Come with me," said a familiar voice. "Quick!"

My heart skipped. The light receded back to the far horizon over the hills. "Frasier?" I whipped around.

My friend was breathing hard. His eyes behind his crooked glasses were huge and his Superboy cape was tugged half around his neck. Out of breath, he pointed.

A little ways ahead, a knot of adults was bending over something on the ground. As I watched, more adults stepped out of the moving column. No, they didn't step, really. It was like they got to that point and were yanked out. They closed in around the struggling figure on the ground.

"It's Jessie," panted Frasier. "They've got her. Come on!"

Jessie! Panic seized me. What were they doing to her? "Leave her alone!" I shrieked as we raced toward the growing huddle of adults. "Get away from her!"

They paid no attention to us. More dropped out of

line. They crowded together, hip to hip, shoulder to shoulder. We couldn't even see Jessie any more.

"Move," shouted Frasier, shoving at an old man.

"Out of my way," I yelled, shoving nice Mrs. Stowe as hard as I could.

But they didn't budge. They didn't even seem to know we were there. The people made a solid, immovable wall around my sister. We kept pushing and shoving and yelling, but we couldn't get through.

Suddenly all of them bent forward at once. A murmur went up from them but we couldn't make out what it was. All we could hear was Jessie's piercing but shaky voice. "Let me go, you creeps!" she demanded. "Let me go! Let me go!"

Suddenly all the adults stood up together. As if thinking with one mind. They had lifted Jessie off the ground. She was balanced on their shoulders. Some held her ankles, more of them held her arms, and another bunch supported her back. Jessie could barely wriggle, although even in the dark we could see her straining and struggling.

"Noooooooooooooo," she screamed as they began to move forward, rejoining the line and carrying her off.

Frasier and I screamed, too, as we punched and pummeled their backs, jumping up to try and get a hold of Jessie's foot or her ankle. If we could only reach her, we thought, we could save her. But the adults were too tall and there were too many of them.

We rained blows on their shoulders and backs, but they didn't feel a thing. They just kept going. Jessie went quiet. I hoped she was just saving her strength for struggling.

And then we could hear what the adults were chanting.

"Bring-her-to-the-light," they were saying all together. "To-the-liiiiight."

Frasier and I looked at each other in horror. "We have to do something," said Frasier. "We have to find a way."

"Let's try tackling them," I suggested.

Frasier nodded. We bent down, braced ourselves, then hurtled forward, cannoning into them with all our might. The wall of bodies wavered, sagged, and then straightened, going on with hardly a ripple.

My chest felt hollow with fright and dread. "Maybe we can wedge our way through," I said desperately. "Push in between two of them and then fight from the inside."

Dark as it was, I could see Frasier go pale. "But then they'll have us, too," he said. "There are so many of them."

"Yes," I said. "But they're not strong. One-on-one we're stronger than they are. Mrs. Pringle's hands were hardly more than cobwebs on me. I know we can fight them. Besides, we have to try."

Frasier nodded. "Okay. Let's do it."

I tried to think of myself as an arrow. Holding my hands together in front of me like a diver, I aimed for a crack between two of the people. Then I threw myself between them as hard as I could. I could feel the shock wave as Frasier did the same.

For a second I felt the bodies give, and then it seemed as if the whole wall of people felt us and pushed back. Frasier and I just popped out again and landed on the ground.

But Frasier looked excited. "I think I've got it," he said, pushing his glasses back up his nose. "They're not like separate people, right? They act like one organism, responding to everything together. That's the only way they're strong enough to pick up Jessie and carry her. We've been going at it all wrong, attacking their strength, not their weakness."

Frasier was right. They didn't look or act like individuals. And from here on the ground the organism they most looked like was a giant centipede. For a second, almost hypnotized, I watched their legs, shuffling along in step. I felt my own excitement growing as I saw what Frasier meant.

"Their legs," I said, jumping up.

Frasier grinned. "You've got it! You take one side and I'll take the other."

"Let's go." Energy was coursing through my veins once again.

I picked the tallest man on my side, and when Frasier yelled, "Ready!" I darted in, grabbed his foot and yanked it off the ground.

A shudder went through the human centipede.

"Yes!" yelled Frasier, and I glanced sideways to see him step backwards with a foot in his hands. We grinned at each other and held on. I could feel the foot I was holding jerk as if it was still walking. The man's other foot hopped, faltered, buckled.

The "centipede" lurched one way, then the other. The man toppled to the ground, knocking two others down with him like dominoes. I let go, quickly grabbing another foot and jerking it up. In an instant, it seemed, the "centipede" fell apart and was nothing more than a confused mass of churning legs and tangled bodies.

"Jessie!" I called, gingerly picking my way through the confusion.

"Here, I'm here!"

I hardly recognized my sister's voice. She sounded so hoarse and worn out. But I saw her familiar figure rising from the tangle. She hopped and jumped in panicky little steps, trying not to touch any of the people who'd held her captive.

Frasier and I reached her at the same time and hoisted her over the scissoring legs. "They think they're still walking," said Frasier wonderingly.

Jessie shuddered, then kept shuddering. "I *know* those people," she said. "It's like their bodies are there but they're not."

It sounded confusing, but I knew exactly what she meant. These zombies were only the shells of people we knew. Something else was making them behave like this. Something not human.

Once we were out of range, we slumped down against a boulder to catch our breath. "We've got to get Jessie out of here," whispered Frasier, wrapping himself in his Superboy cape and rubbing his bristly hair thoughtfully. "For some reason, whatever is out there really wants her. It's too strong now for us to stop it."

"No way," said Jessie sharply. "We have to save our parents." She pointed at the shambling line of people. "We're going to stop whatever is doing this."

"Unless they stop us first," muttered Frasier into his cape.

Jessie ignored him, staring fiercely at the light glowing ever more threateningly from the clouds over Harley Hill.

"For some reason, it can't seem to take over our minds," I said quietly. "I think we're the only ones who *can* stop it."

"Suggestions?" asked Frasier, his voice cracking.

"We go to the source," I said. "To the light."

"Then what?" asked Frasier hopelessly.

"We'll figure that out when we get there," I said, standing up and dusting off my jeans.

We walked back to where we'd left our bikes. All the adults were gone now, even the ones who'd had Jessie. We could just see the last of the line of sleepwalkers, snaking down through a cut between hills.

119

As I hopped onto my bike, I felt the hum in the earth start up again. It startled me. I hadn't noticed when we'd stopped feeling it. But now it seemed stronger than ever.

There was a dull, heavy feeling in my chest as we headed into the Harley Hills. Something was up there. Something not of this earth.

And somehow I knew what it wanted.

Us.

31

"There it is," I said softly, a fist clamping around my heart. "The source."

We were at the top of a rise just before the triple peaks of the Harley Hills. The glowing light was brighter here and the clouds billowed over one another like steam in a witch's cauldron.

"That's the same spot where the lightning struck during the weird storm," said Frasier, pointing to a dark shadowy area just below the middle peak of the Harley Hills. "I think this is trouble."

I nodded, remembering the strange beauty of the star-shaped charred patch that marked the lightning strike. It was different now. Emanating from its center was a cold white light. The light was steady, but it seemed to cast long, flickering shadows that licked at the hillside as if tasting it.

"What is it?" Frasier asked in a hushed voice.

"Looks like the opening to a cave," I said, my mind searching for reasonable explanations.

"Or an old mine," Jessie suggested. "There used to be mines in these hills a long time ago. Maybe the lightning from those clouds opened one up again."

"Yeah? Gold mines?" asked Frasier, sounding interested.

"Nah," I said, remembering stories about the old mines. "It was something boring like potassium or zinc."

"Mmm," mused Frasier. "I suppose it could be an old mine shaft blasted open by lightning. But what's making it glow from inside?"

As I was trying to think of an answer, the light got stronger. It began to pulsate and throb like a beating heart.

"There's something in there," I said, my own heart beginning to flutter. "Something alive!"

We watched as the light pulsed, casting long erratic shadows outside the opening.

"It may be alive," Frasier said grimly. "But it's not human."

He started to back away, pulling his cape up over his head to shut out the glow.

"Where are you going?" demanded Jessie.

"Home." Frasier sounded determined.

"Don't you get it?" said Jessie, wheeling on him. "Whatever this thing is, it's got control of our parents. We can't go home anymore!"

"They're parents," said Frasier. "They'll know what to do."

"You've seen them, Frasier," I said. "They're not acting like parents or even like grown-ups. They're not themselves anymore. They can't help us. They can't even help themselves."

Just then, a movement far below caught our eyes. The line of adults had come into view. They were still shuffling along, one after the other, winding around a low hill like a column of ants. They were headed straight for Harley Hills.

Jessie scowled at him. "If it were the other way around and this were happening to us kids, do you think our parents would just go home and leave us here?"

Frasier sighed deeply. "No, definitely not," he said. He stood up, breathed deep, and straightened his cape, squaring his shoulders. "Well, what are you guys waiting for?" he asked, jumping on his bike.

Frasier headed right for the Harley Hills and the cave that hadn't been there until tonight, his Superboy cape flying out behind him.

32

Pedaling down the ridge as hard as we could go, we built up speed for the ride into the hills. Frasier was in the lead, but this time he didn't mess around riding up the charred area of the original lightning strike.

We steered clear of the burned rock even though this other way was steeper. Finally it got so steep we couldn't ride. We left our bikes below the opening to the cave.

"Here goes nothing," Frasier said, touching his Superboy cape for luck.

Cautiously, we climbed up to the cave opening. As we got closer, the light seemed to pulse brighter and faster as if it were aware of us and excited — or maybe frightened — by our presence.

Normally I'm pretty brave but right then I was terrified. Scared witless. My insides gurgled as if everything inside my skin had turned to water.

"Wow," said Frasier as we pulled ourselves over the last ridge and stood at last before the cave opening. "It certainly isn't any natural cave, and it definitely isn't a *human* mine shaft."

The opening to the glowing cave was as tall as a big man and was almost round. It spiraled into the hill as if a giant corkscrew had burrowed into the rock. Frasier walked right up to the cave, gazing around in amazement. He ran his hand along the edge of one of the spirals. The chewed-up rock was melted, the edge smooth and glassy.

"Awesome," said Frasier, kneeling to get a closer look. "It looks like it got blasted by a giant laser."

"Maybe it was lightning," said Jessie doubtfully, walking up behind Frasier. The glow of the cold light fell on her, making her skin look as pale as white marble while her eyes flashed with sparks. I shivered, not knowing if it was fear or the chill of the night air that made me shudder.

"I don't think lightning can melt rock," I said, trying to peer into the cave without getting too close. But I couldn't see more than a few feet inside despite the light. Either the glow was too bright or the cave tunnel took a turn that hid most of it from view. From the entrance it was impossible to tell.

"Definitely not lightning," announced Frasier, getting to his feet. He turned a glassy, fist-sized rock over and

125

over in his hands. "Something much hotter than lightning did this. Lightning can't bore a hole into the earth. Not this deep."

"We'll have to explore it," said Jessie.

"We'll go together," said Frasier, looking eager and scared at the same time.

"No," said Jessie. "What if it's a trap? Two of us should stay outside while one of us checks it out. You two stay. I'll shout when it's okay to come in."

Before we could stop her she darted into the cave mouth, into the light. I squinted after her, trying to shade my eyes with my hand, but she disappeared from view.

I bit my lip anxiously. Jessie was as brave as anybody twice her size. I knew that. But I couldn't help wondering if whatever it was that had made the cave was also drawing her into it. The strange light wanted Jessie. I was sure of it. I had to go after her.

But as I started forward, the ground shook. A tingling sensation traveled from my feet up my legs and my back, right to my head. It was the hum. We'd been hearing or feeling it for so long we'd almost forgotten it.

But suddenly it was louder and stronger. The throbbing vibration began to pulse in time with the light, which was growing brighter. What was happening? Had the light got my twin sister?

The hum jangled my bones and made my stomach queasy. The light was so bright I couldn't see a foot into the cave. The vibration made my anxiety seem even worse. I felt like I was going to explode.

Then suddenly a voice spoke to us out of the light.

33

"Comecomcomcominininininininitsssitsssitsss-cooooooloooooooolooooool."

Frasier's eyes goggled behind his glasses. My heart pounded. "What was that?" said Frasier.

The voice started up again. "Guyuyuyuysss!"

"It's Jessie!" I burst out, dashing into the entrance.

Frasier was right behind me. "Must be an echo," he said. "Her voice is echoing off all these spirals. She doesn't sound hurt or anything. I don't think," he added.

"Listen!" I demanded as Jessie's voice started up again. The echo was much less distorting inside the cave, and we could make out what she was saying.

"Come on guys," she was calling out. "It's cool!"

"We're coming!" I yelled back.

Inside the cave the walls and ceiling curved in' a thickly ridged spiral. The glassy rock glowed pink and gold with traces of a darker blue. It was beautiful but creepy, too. What had made this place?

The continuing hum from the cave floor made our feet tingle. It was almost an electrical feeling.

The light was glowing from deep inside the tunnel. We felt ourselves drawn to it. Slowly we crept forward, going deeper inside.

My sneakers skidded on the slick surface and I almost fell. Frasier was right there to grab me. "Careful," he said. "I don't think it's a good idea to break a leg in here."

Jessie was waiting for us as we cautiously navigated the first curve of the tunnel. A warm breeze coming from under the earth stirred the hairs on my arms, making me realize I was trembling. It wasn't cold, but I was shivering.

"Smell that?" asked Jessie. There were diamond bright gleams in her eyes.

I sniffed. The breeze was carrying some kind of scent. Strange but not unpleasant. Kind of familiar.

"It's spicy," said Frasier.

"Yeah, like cinnamon," Jessie said.

"Maybe they're baking pies down here," joked Frasier, laughing nervously. "Heh-heh-heh."

"Sure. And we're the main ingredient," quipped Jessie, tossing her head.

"My turn to lead," I said and slipped past Jessie. I was trying to remember what the cinnamon smell reminded me of. But it wouldn't come to me.

We crept along in silence for a while, following the

spiraling walls into the hillside. The light wasn't getting any closer, and we all seemed to sense it was a good idea not to make any noise.

The tunnel was narrow, only wide enough for us to walk single file. I felt my shoulders hunching with tension. We were deep inside the rocky hill, and I imagined the immense weight of the hills towering over us. There was nothing to protect us from being crushed but the walls of this strange cave.

I looked back to check on the others. Jessie was right behind me, tight-lipped. Her shoulders were hunched, too, I noticed, and she gave the walls quick, fearful glances. Frasier was hanging slightly back, his Superboy cape wrapped tight around him, his glasses winking and flashing in the cave light.

He looked almost funny, a big nerd in a costume cape, his eyes bugged out behind the glasses. But I knew he was tough and I was glad to have him there covering our backs. Frasier would never break and run in a panic like some kids would.

A few minutes later Jessie touched my shoulder. I stopped and looked at her questioningly. "Feel that?" she whispered, laying her hand on the cave wall.

I put my hand beside hers. My palm tingled and I jerked it away. The hum was coming through the stone. It was on all sides of us now. "Check it out," urged Jessie.

Frasier and I both placed our hands flat on the wall, trying not to flinch away. "It's pulsing," breathed Frasier.

There was a rhythm to it. *Bump-de-bump. Bump-de-bump.* "What is it?" asked Frasier. "Code again? Like Morse?"

I frowned, feeling something nagging at me. Something I should know. "It feels, sounds — familiar," I said.

Jessie nodded. Her dark eyes were huge. "It's like a heartbeat," she said.

And I felt my own heart lurch. *Bump-de-bump.*

34

With the hum magnifying our own heartbeats, our feet felt heavy, like lead. As we entered yet another curve just like all the others, I started thinking maybe we should go back. Before it was too late.

But as we rounded the curve, I forgot about leaving, forgot about the heartbeat in the walls.

The tunnel opened into a huge cavernous area. The rock walls glittered. Strange stalactite formations hung over our heads, some almost to the cave floor.

The light still came from somewhere beyond and threw long snaky shadows across the floor and walls.

"Wow!" Frasier's cape rippled in the breeze as he threw back his head, looking around eagerly. He walked over to one of the stalactites and looked it over. Then he whipped off his glasses and squinted, his nose an inch from the weird spike.

"This isn't rock! It's metal," he announced excitedly. "Or metal that's been melted into the rock."

"What?" I moved around the stalactite, looking it over without getting too close. It did have an odd, silvery sheen to it, like steel maybe. "That's impossible."

"Think about it, man." Frasier's eyes were feverish with excitement, his fear momentarily forgotten. "What if an alien spacecraft really did land in the Harley Hills? What if it was going so fast it kind of *melted* through the rock and stone?"

I looked down the cavern through the pattern of heavy stalactites that hung like huge airplane struts from the ceiling and walls. "You really believe that?" I asked, resisting the idea. My brain scrambled for a better explanation. "There's such a thing as rock that looks like gold, you know. Maybe this is rock that looks like metal. It was probably a zinc mine once. That's what it is. Zinc."

Frasier shrugged, the cape flaring out behind him. "I don't know what to believe," he said softly.

"Hey, guys," called Jessie. "Come on! I think I see something." She was half hidden behind a sharp stalactite, moving in the direction of the light.

We hurried to catch up, saying no more about alien spaceships. Jessie wove through the "struts" extruding from the rock, moving purposefully.

The glow was getting brighter and brighter, hurting my eyes and making me blink. The hum was so loud my head buzzed and I couldn't hear myself think. The spicy smell filled my nostrils, swam into my lungs, and settled in my stomach. I felt dizzy.

Suddenly it popped into my brain what the cinnamon smell reminded me of. It smelled like the rain had tasted the night of the weird storm.

I swallowed, trying to keep the fear from bubbling up through my throat in a scream. I knew we should turn around and run as fast as we could out of here. But if we did, then nothing would ever be the same. Life would never be "perfectly normal" again.

I fought down my panic as best I could, stumbling along behind Jessie. But just when I thought I couldn't stand another minute, the cave ended.

We were standing in front of a high solid wall. It was silvery gray, made out of the same metallic stuff as the stalactite "struts." But it was smooth and glowing. The whole wall pulsed with light.

My hand reached up like it didn't belong to me and touched the glowing surface. It was cool and smooth. Smooth like skin. I jerked my hand away — could it be alive? Was this the alien, buried deep inside the rock?

"I found it," Frasier said quietly. I wasn't sure I heard him right over the hum in my head.

"Found what?"

"A way inside. Where the light is coming from."

35

Down near the cave floor, almost hidden in shadow, was a small slotlike opening. It was just big enough for a kid to crawl through.

"I don't know about this," I said, down on my hands and knees trying to peer through. My knees were quaking against the floor.

"We've come this far," said Jessie. "We can't turn back now. Think of Mom and Dad. They're out there somewhere, and we're the only ones that can save them."

She was right. I poked my head through the opening before I could think about it any more. A glow came up from beneath me. I wriggled through and, as I pulled my foot in, my knee slipped into nothingness.

I jerked back against the wall, my heart pounding against my ribs at the near disaster. "Careful," I whispered sharply to Jessie who was next through. "There's nothing here but a narrow, clifflike ledge. Scrunch over by me. And warn Frasier."

When we were all safely huddled on the ledge, we looked around in amazement. Over us the metallic wall arched in a huge curved dome, perfectly smooth. Jessie coughed. The cinnamonlike smell was so strong here our eyes were watering.

Carefully I peered over to look below our ledge. I shuddered to see what I had almost fallen into. Just a foot or so below the ledge was a huge pool of glowing metallic liquid.

"This is where the light is coming from," whispered Jessie in awe.

"And the hum, too, I think," I said, feeling it reverberate against my heart.

As the shimmering surface vibrated, ripples passed over it in strange patterns. There were swirls, almost whirlpools, and circles that spread across the surface in low waves. Other ripples marched across the pool in straight lines, lapping against the curved wall.

Under the surface, inside the glow, I thought I saw something move. Was it swimming? I blinked away the water that the spice kept bringing to my eyes, but I still couldn't get a clear look. Maybe it was my imagination. Then I saw it again, like a shadow that came almost to the surface then dipped away.

"I think it's alive," said Frasier reverently.

"What are you talking about?" I snapped, fear making me sound irritated.

"What were you expecting?" Frasier shot back. "Little green men?"

"You mean you think the liquid itself is alive?" asked Jessie.

Frasier shifted, pulling at his cape as if it were too tight on his neck. "The liquid. Or something growing inside it," he said.

Jessie stretched out on her stomach and stuck her head over. "I wonder what it feels like." Her hand reached over the ledge.

"Don't!" I cried, grabbing for her wrist.

But it was too late.

36

As Frasier and I watched in horror, Jessie's finger dipped into the pool. "Ooh, it's thick and icky," she said. "Like warm Jell-O."

Suddenly the light pulsed in a bright flash around her finger. The liquid surged up in a blob, slurping onto her hand. The blob formed dark tentacles which instantly wound around her fingers. Suckers glommed onto her skin.

"Noooooo!"

Jessie screamed and jerked backwards, shaking her hand violently. The tentacles flew from her fingers and spattered on the wall behind us. Frasier seemed paralyzed.

I crawled over him. Grabbing Jessie's shoulders, I shoved her toward the opening. "Go!" I yelled. "Hurry!"

I looked over my shoulder. The spatters on the wall were moving, inching together like worms, re-forming.

The pool was bubbling excitedly. More tentacles

began to form and heave themselves up out of the water. Most rose only a few inches and fell back to try again but some hit the side of the pool and began to ooze up toward us rapidly.

Jessie shot through the opening. I shook Frasier, who was still staring into the pool, mesmerized. "Snap out of it!" I shouted, digging my hand into his shoulder.

He blinked. Life came back into his eyes. "Yaaaaiiiiii," he screamed. "Let's get out of here!"

Tentacles wiggled up over the edge of our narrow shelf, tips waving in the air, seeking us. I threw myself into the opening, but panic made everything seem slow. My shoulder stuck. Unable to see behind me, I pictured the slimy tentacle winding around my ankle, pulling me back.

"Hurry up!" yelled Frasier, his voice squeaky with terror.

With a hefty push from Frasier I rammed myself through and spilled out on the other side. Quickly I twisted around to help Frasier. He was bigger than me. Could he get through all right?

"Take it easy, Fraze," said Jessie, kneeling in front of the opening. "If you shove too hard you'll get stuck. Turn a little sideways — that's it."

Frasier's head appeared in the opening, his face beet red with effort. He was concentrating, wriggling through carefully like Jessie said. But his eyes were bugging out with fear. I knew he was having the same thought I'd had — picturing those monster tentacles sneaking along where he couldn't see them, grabbing his ankle and pulling him back, back into the pool.

Frasier's shoulders were through, and I breathed a sigh of relief. That was the hard part. Now Jessie and I could just pull him the rest of the way.

But suddenly Frasier's mouth stretched so wide I could almost see down into his stomach. At first no sound came out but his eyes bugged out with terror. He gasped like a fish a couple of times, then said, "It's got me."

Jessie and I each grabbed a shoulder, but we couldn't hold on. Frasier was yanked back through the opening so fast his Superboy cape flipped over his head. We gripped the end of the cape and pulled, but we could still feel our friend slipping away.

"Brace your feet against the wall," I told Jessie, flipping onto my back and pulling on that cape with every bit of strength I had, using my feet as leverage against the metallic wall.

"It's working!" cried Jessie.

It was true. I felt Frasier slide back toward us an inch, then another. A moment later his hand appeared, gripping the edge of the opening. We could hear him grunting with the effort to pull himself free. I grabbed one hand, Jessie grabbed the other, and, still keeping our feet braced, we dragged him back through.

As his feet appeared I could see a long, glistening

tentacle wrapped around his legs. It was stretching thinner and thinner like an overstretched rubber band, and then suddenly — *POP!* The tentacle broke and snapped back through the opening.

Frasier collapsed at our feet. "Whew," he said, his chest heaving. "I thought I was a goner."

"Look out!" yelled Jessie.

I whirled around and saw it.

A newer, shinier, bigger blob was oozing through the opening. It was nearly as big around as we were. As we watched for an instant, paralyzed with horror, it began to form suckers, like a giant tentacle. It was getting bigger.

And it was coming to get us.

37

The tip of the tentacle paused at the edge of the opening. It waved in the air, seeking us.

Correction. Seeking Jessie. The instant it sensed her, the tentacle shot forward. I threw myself into the air and tackled Jessie, shoving her back the way we'd come. "Run!" I yelled, and we were running before the word was out of my mouth, our feet scarcely touching the ground.

The hum in the air rumbled in our chests, trying to slow us down. As we passed under the stalactite "struts" in the cavern, I risked a look back. The blob, now a fully streamlined tentacle, was stretching after us, weaving through the struts like a monster snake.

It was only a quick glance, but it looked to me like the stalactites were dripping silvery drops onto the tentacle. Like the thing was growing by melting the metallic rock.

We reached the corkscrew tunnel. The stretching

tentacle was only a little ways behind us and seemed to be getting closer every time I dared to glance behind me. I tried not to think how far we'd come into the hill.

We kept running.

I could hear Jessie and Frasier panting and knew their lungs were aching just like mine. The muscles in my legs were burning. How far had we come? Every turn looked the same, the walls gleaming and glassy smooth.

The tentacle was getting thinner as it followed, reaching out, trying to grab us. Now it was no bigger around than my leg. But it was still gaining. I wasn't sure how much farther we could run. Breath rasped in my throat. My heart banged in my chest.

We skidded around another curve. Frasier slipped and almost fell. He stumbled on without looking back, his cape streaming straight out behind him.

The tentacle raced closer, its suckers reaching, reaching. It was so thin I could almost see through it, like a hungry gummy bear. It was only inches behind me, straining for my neck. The little hairs on the back of my neck rose, sensing it.

I felt it brush me.

With no breath for screaming, I somehow put on a burst of speed. Suddenly, above the hum that never stopped, there was a *Plop! Pop!* I glanced around and saw the tentacle, stretched thinner than my little finger, snap backwards and disappear back into the tunnel.

And there, right ahead of us, was the cave opening and the night sky. We'd made it! We were safe!

Or were we?

Frasier groaned. "Look!" he cried with the last of his breath.

38

We collapsed on the ground and looked down. Up the charred side of the hill came the long, slow line of adults. They weaved and staggered mindlessly up the scorched path. But there was no doubt about where they were headed. They were coming right toward us, right toward the mouth of the cave.

They were heading for the light. And the grasp of those hungry tentacles.

"We've got to do something," Jessie cried, jumping up as if she hadn't just been running for her life.

"Yes," I said wearily. "But what?"

Frasier snapped his fingers. "I've got it," he announced, pushing up his glasses. "Gravity!"

"Huh?"

"Follow me." Frasier started scrambling up the hill alongside the cave entrance. Jessie and I looked at each other. She was as puzzled as I was. But a lot of Frasier's ideas were good ones, if they weren't just plain wacky. So we followed.

There was a rocky slope above the mouth of the cave. Frasier stood, hands on hips, surveying the area. "This is a good one," he said, walking over to a boulder that was as tall as we were. He got behind it and put his shoulder to the rock. "Come on, guys! Let's push it."

"Push it where?" asked Jessie, sounding annoyed. "What are you doing?"

"Avalanche," said Frasier as if it should be obvious. "I read all about them in a book I had on volcanoes and earthquakes. See those smaller boulders in front of this one?"

We nodded.

"All we need to do is work up some momentum, and this big boulder will do the rest of the work for us. Ready?" Frasier regarded us impatiently. "We don't have all night."

Jessie and I crowded up next to him behind the boulder and heaved. Nothing happened. We heaved again with all our strength. The boulder rocked about half an inch. Then stopped. It was just too heavy for us.

Dejected, we stepped back to rest for a second. Then my eye fell on a scraggly tree. "Yes!" I shouted, running toward the tree. "A lever. We can use a branch as a lever."

"Good idea," beamed Frasier, hurrying to help me rip

a branch off the tree. It took three of us to break it and we felt precious seconds speeding past, but finally we got the end of the branch under the boulder. Jessie found a flat stone to lever it against, and we were ready to try again.

Jessie pushed all her weight down on the branch while Frasier and I pushed the boulder. It groaned, it rocked, rocked again and slowly, slowly, it began to roll.

We jumped back and the boulder took off, gathering speed, dislodging everything in its path. The ground shook under our feet. We scurried around, pushing smaller boulders after it. Others bounced and began to roll on their own. Small stones went cascading down the slope. Soon it seemed every rock, big and small, on the whole slope was moving downhill toward the edge.

And then, with a great crash, our rockfall heaved itself over the edge. Rock dust filled the air. We breathed it in, enjoying the dirt-clean smell of it after the clinging spiciness of the cave. And when the noise settled, we ran to the edge and looked over.

"*YES!*" We slapped five and danced around laughing.

The cave entrance was completely blocked. No light penetrated through our rock wall. The glow from the clouds was fading fast. Even the strange clouds were dissolving and blowing away in wisps.

We had done it! We won!

"We've got to find Mom and Dad," said Jessie, catching her breath. "Somehow we've got to get them back home and find a way to wake them."

"Right." We picked our way back down the hill toward the sound of the grown-ups' crunching footsteps.

"I'm going to check out our avalanche," said Frasier. "Make sure it'll really work."

While Frasier went to inspect our rockslide, Jessie and I headed further down the slope. But as we approached the zombie adults, we saw something odd. They weren't walking in a straight line anymore. They were wandering around in all directions. Some of the people just picked a rock to sit on and looked around them in bewilderment.

"They're themselves again," cried Jessie joyfully. "They woke up!"

It was true. There was life in their faces once more. "What am I doing here?" we heard one lady say to herself in a normal voice, scratching her head.

"How did I get here?" asked somebody else. "What are you doing here, Steve?" another man said to his neighbor.

Mrs. Pringle laid her hand on my arm. I snatched it away and jumped about a foot. She looked at me quizzically. "You children are out awfully late, aren't you? Where are your parents?"

"Good question," I muttered, edging away from her.

"Nick! Jessie!" It was Mom's voice!

"There you are," said Dad. "We've been looking all over for you. We were so worried we had to get up a search party."

All around him adults began to nod, seizing on his words as a perfect explanation for what they were doing out at Harley Hills in the middle of the night. "Yes," they chorused. "You kids had us worried to death."

Jessie rolled her eyes so only I could see.

"I can't believe it but I think we're going to get grounded again," she said.

I laughed with her. It was so good to see our parents acting normal again. I didn't care if they made us stay in all summer. "Coming Mom and Dad. We just have to get Frasier."

Mom sighed. "Well, hurry up. It's late."

I ran back up to the cave mouth. As I looked up at the pile of rocks, I started to feel uneasy. Sure, the adults were themselves again but it wasn't really over, was it? We'd blocked the cave, but the glowing creature was still alive under Harley Hill.

Frasier was sitting on a rock, looking up at our avalanche. I went over to him. "The thing is still in there," I said. "It won't really be over until it's gone, will it?"

Frasier didn't answer.

I wondered how long it would take the tentacled aliens to pick and ooze their way out through the avalanche and come after us again.

"We'll have to find some way to get rid of them," I said. "Any ideas, Fraze?"

My friend slowly looked up at me. There was a strange look in his eyes behind the thick glasses — a secretive gleam. He got up and started to walk down the hill. There was something different about his walk, too. His legs seemed stiff and he planted his feet heavily with every step.

"Frasier," I called after him. "What's wrong?"

He turned slowly and smiled at me. "Wrong? Nothing-is-wrong," he said in a flat robotic voice. "Everything-is-perfectly-normal."

I stared, shocked speechless. My best friend had been taken over by the aliens!